THE FINAL GAMBIT

MITCH HERRON 9

STEVE P. VINCENT

1

———

Mitch Herron walked through the dense trees, a rifle in one hand and a fishing pole in the other. For once, he wasn't concerned about stealth and didn't mind the snap of the dry twigs beneath his feet, each akin to a gunshot in the otherwise whisper-quiet forest. He'd been wandering for hours, keen to return to the lake he'd found a few days prior, a place that had helped clear his mind of the chaos of the world.

Emerging from the tree line and catching his first glimpse of the serene water, he couldn't help but pause in awe. Although it was cold, it was a nice day, and the lake's surface was a deep shade of blue, mirroring the sky above. The water itself was calm, the gentle breeze causing only a few ripples. He made his way down to the water's edge and gazed down at his reflection, seeing a man he hardly recognized.

A worn and weathered face marked by years of violence and darkness... but, deep in his eyes, there was a glimmer of hope and a sense of purpose.

He took a deep breath, savoring the fresh scent of the forest, a place of tranquillity he'd discovered only a few hours away from the other place of refuge in his life: the forest shack he'd shared with Erica Kearns for the last few weeks. That too had become a place of rare happiness for Herron. They'd spent long days making their place a little nicer, and long nights in each other's arms.

It was an experience he'd always remember, even though what had brought him to this moment were things he would prefer to forget.

A month ago, Herron had had a close call with his most fearsome enemy, the former Enclave assassin Shade. After coming close to death at the hands of his nemesis several times, Herron had finally gained the advantage and been ready to end Shade once and for all... but in choosing to save the love of his life, he had let the killer walk. The choice haunted him, but the life he looked forward to forging with Kearns salved a wound that would otherwise have festered.

His fight was over.

He'd served the U.S. Government as a soldier, the Enclave as a cold-blooded killer, and various governments since as an involuntary asset. He'd killed criminals, drug runners, corrupt generals, and world leaders, but also more than his share of innocents, a fact he would carry with him to the grave. He could only hope that when the tally of his life was finalized, the good he'd done in recent years outweighed the bad.

He and Kearns had agreed that they would stay in the forest, making the best life they could in the shack, for as long as they needed to. In time, they might be able to come out of hiding, to stake out a normal life somewhere Kearns could work, once again using her exceptional scientific talents to benefit humanity. As for him, he could live without having to look over his shoulder every waking moment. But that prospect was a long way off from being reality; for now, there were too many individuals and governments who considered him public enemy number one.

People who'd use his newfound love for Kearns to get to him.

After the final battle with Shade, Herron and Kearns had sought medical help in Baltimore, using a backroom doctor who owed Herron a favor and could be trusted. He'd patched up both their wounds, making sure to let them know how lucky Kearns was to still be alive: had Shade's gunshot taken her another inch to the left, she'd have been in real trouble. As it was, she'd have a scar and a memory.

Then, at last, they'd headed for their forest hideaway to begin the long process of healing and connecting.

With a sigh, Herron tried to put such thoughts of the past aside, even for a few hours. Now he had a more pressing challenge: catching some fish. Canned foods made up most of their shack's stores, and while they'd planted some seeds, it would take time for the vegetables to grow. In the meantime, Herron was forced to hunt and fish for most of what they needed.

He looked around the span of the lake and listened, trying to sense any threat or disturbance. Satisfied there was none, he rested the rifle against a tree near the water, then shrugged his backpack off his shoulders. Working efficiently, he removed his fishing supplies and bait from inside the bag and prepared his rod. Then, ready to begin, he cast a line out into the water and sat in the dirt to wait.

Time passed, the lake in no hurry to provide him the protein he sought. Herron wasn't sure if it was a commentary on his skills as an angler or the abundance of the fish beneath the surface, but the dozen or so times he'd come here, he'd never returned empty-handed. Anyway, it wasn't like he had anywhere else to be. Kearns was resting, still recovering from her wound, and all his other chores for the day were done.

While he waited for the nibble of a fish and the battle for his dinner to start, he made sure to enjoy the serenity. For weeks, he hadn't seen another person except Kearns, hadn't heard any other sign of humanity. It was like they were the last survivors on Earth, a scenario they'd joked about the previous night, huddled next to the fire.

The thought was still fresh in his mind when the whir of a helicopter in the distance broke the silence. It was approaching fast, and Herron's mind worked to determine whether the chopper was slowing or just passing over the forest.

It was slowing.

Dropping the fishing rod, Herron got to his feet and grabbed the rifle. Confident he wouldn't have to do any shooting but prepared to unleash hell if he needed to, he chambered a round. As a further precaution, he retreated into the tree line and had only just made it when the chopper came into view. Small and black, it lacked any sort of markings – a combo of traits that usually spelled trouble.

"Fuck," Herron muttered, and took aim at the helicopter, willing it to keep on with its journey.

But it was hovering over the lake now, the downdraft from the rotors sending waves out across the previously serene surface, and it clearly wasn't leaving. Herron weighed up the danger to himself and Kearns. They were isolated, off-grid, and had told nobody where they were going. Anyone coming at them with so much heavy metal likely had hostile intentions.

He fired.

The round pinged harmlessly off the helicopter's landing strut, exactly as Herron had intended. He didn't want to kill anyone or bring the bird down – for now. What he did want was to make it clear to those aboard the chopper that he knew they were there, and that if they didn't go away there'd be a fight.

The next shot wouldn't be a warning.

Nothing happened immediately; then the rear door of the chopper opened. Herron spotted a pair of black-clad men with automatic weapons an instant before their return gunfire tore into the trees. Abandoning the large oak he was behind, he retreated deeper into the cover of the trees. A few times, he popped out to take another shot, but his bolt-action rifle was meant for hunting game, not tangling with enemies rocking full auto.

The chopper flew a little closer, disgorging more armed men on zip lines as the original pair kept up the gunfire. Herron thought more about running for it, escaping into the denser parts of the forest and away from the shoreline, where he was at both a numerical and mobility disadvantage.

But a voice over a loudspeaker changed his mind.

"Herron, it's me," a familiar female said. "We're not

here to hurt you, but if you keep shooting, then we're going to have to start aiming at you instead of the trees."

Herron's eyes narrowed. Taking the time to look now, he could see that while the trees around him had been shredded by bullets, all the shots had gone high – much higher than any standing human. The shooters had been trying to suppress him, keep him on the back foot, while the ground team had been getting into position.

Why?

The voice belonged to Zoe, an MI6 agent Herron had helped – and been helped by – in recent months. It had been an alliance of convenience, broken when Herron had walked away from a deal they'd made. He'd hoped Zoe – like Shade – would walk away and give up on finding him, but it looked like she was here to collect what was owed.

"Throw the rifle out where I can see it, then I'll land in so we can have a chat," Zoe announced. "Force me to root you out, and there'll be consequences for you *and* for Kearns."

Zoe had played her trump card, and they both knew it.

Herron had little choice but to comply. With the shack an hour away on foot, even if he could deal with the shooters here, he couldn't guarantee there wasn't a second team, waiting there for the word from Zoe to strike.

Once again, Kearns' safety overrode his desire to shoot his way out of a tricky situation.

Still sheltered behind a tree and protected from any incoming fire that might start up again, he held his rifle out and tossed it onto the ground, hoping the attackers could see his act of surrender. A few seconds later, he emerged, hands away from his body so it was clear he wasn't reaching for a weapon.

It worked: despite his exposed position, nobody filled him with lead.

He waited, frozen in place, as Zoe's operatives advanced with their weapons leveled. She had said they wouldn't fire upon him, but he knew every operative worth their salt wouldn't hesitate if they believed they or their squad mates were threatened. While he let them approach and scoop up the rifle, however, he shrugged off the man who tried to grab his arm.

"Easy, pal. I've said I'll listen to whatever your boss has to say, but touch me again and you'll be eating through a straw for the next month."

The British operative – a big guy, tall and built – gave him a shit-eating, confident grin that told him everything he needed to know. He thought he was in charge, him and his buddies and their helicopter against one disarmed asshole living it up off-grid. If the grin hadn't telegraphed his intentions, the windup sure as hell did: he cocked a fist back and swung at Herron with enough power to level a skyscraper if he connected.

He didn't.

Herron had been coiled to act from the moment the other man had grinned, ready to explode with violence even as his exterior appearance remained unchanged. He struck as fast as a cobra, his body shifting slightly to the left to take him out of range of the punch, while simultaneously bringing his hand up to catch his attacker's fist. His muscles strained to stop the momentum of the blow, but he managed it.

The other man's grin disappeared, replaced by a grim determination to extract his fist from Herron's vise-like grip. He pulled back, but Herron held tight. The operative let his rifle hang by its strap, to bring his other hand into play, but before he could, Herron twisted his trapped wrist towards his torso. Forced to shift his balance or else suffer a broken wrist, the man was robbed of the leverage and balance he needed to try another punch.

"Had enough?" Herron asked, surprised the guy's buddies hadn't jumped on him yet.

"Fuck you," the operative grunted in reply. "You're a dead man."

Herron shrugged, then drove a kick into his balls. Although the tactical gear the operative was wearing would probably include a cup, no protection is total, and not against the force of the kick Herron delivered. The man groaned, as Herron used the grip on his wrist to pull him closer and drive his knee into his head. He let go of the man's wrist, and the asshole dropped like a stone.

Herron watched him fall, then regarded his buddies with curiosity. "Well?"

"They're under orders not to harm you," Zoe said from behind Herron, her voice cold. "I'm not."

Herron turned to face her, ignoring the flunkies now he knew they weren't a threat. "You shouldn't have come here."

"Your girlfriend told us you were out here at the lake," Zoe replied. "She put up a hell of a fight, by the way."

"If you've done anything to hurt her, I'll end you, no matter what the cost."

"If I wanted her – or you – dead, we'd have started shooting the minute we saw you."

"So, what is it then?"

"You know what it is. You made a deal and then fucked off."

Herron couldn't deny it. To find Shade and rescue Kearns, he'd asked Zoe for help. She'd agreed to provide it, in return for Herron securing and handing over cutting-edge surveillance technology Shade had been in the process of selling to foreign governments. Zoe had delivered on her part of the bargain, then Herron had bailed.

"Shade was going to kill Kearns," Herron said. "I did what I had to do. And I'd do it again."

"That's exactly what I wanted to hear, Mitch," Zoe said. "I've got another team watching over her at the shack where you've been playing happy families. My bosses want that technology you promised, so you're going to get your ass after Shade and get it. In the meantime, you can be content in the knowledge that Great Britain will keep your good lady safe."

Herron sneered. "Even if I wanted to help you, I wouldn't have a clue where Shade is. Unless you've got a bead on him, this discussion is pointless. He *wanted* to be found last time, because he wanted to have it out with me, but now? I wouldn't be surprised if he dropped off the grid for weeks, months, years... who the hell knows?"

"I know," she said. "He boarded a flight at Baltimore International Airport a few days ago. Assumed identity, heavy makeup, and all the right papers, so he didn't trigger any border security flags until he was already at his destination."

"Where was he headed?"

"China."

Herron's mind clouded over as he considered the ramifications of her words. If there had been two constants in his life since he'd started work destroying the Enclave, they'd been his efforts to kill Shade and foil China's ambitions. The idea of his mortal enemy being in the country controlled by a regime he'd done more to harm than any man on Earth made his blood boil.

"He's selling the technology to the PRC?"

"We think so. The regime is fighting hard to suppress the protests that have broken out across China after the invasion of Taiwan and the fall of the Great Firewall. The truth is out there, as Fox Mulder used to say, and the locals are pissed. If the regime gets Shade's facial recognition technology, it will harness a billion cell phones across China. An instant, networked way to hunt down any dissidents they want dead."

Herron briefly thought about refusing the job, letting Shade and the CCP find their own destiny while he and Kearns found theirs. But no matter the urge to let it go, a much stronger pull was dragging him back into the fight: an irresistible desire to finish what he'd started, with Shade and the Chinese government both. The fact that Zoe was – once again – holding Kearns' safety over him as a threat really made no difference.

He was going to end this once and for all.

"You had me at hello," he said. "No need to hold harming Kearns over my head."

"I thought you might say that," Zoe said. "Go to China, find Shade, and secure his technology – just as you promised. If you want to kill him in the process, we won't try to stop you."

"I want to see Kearns first," Herron said, crossing his arms over his chest. "And I don't want your goons anywhere near us when I do."

Zoe looked like she might refuse and insist her operatives always stay within earshot. Then, after holding Herron's gaze for a few moments, she relented. "Deal – but if you renege on this one, it'll be fatal for you both."

HERRON HAD ONLY BEEN AWAY from the shack – and from Kearns – for a few hours, but it felt like an eternity. The simple log structure that had housed them for several happy weeks had been polluted by the presence of an intruding force, popping the bubble of delusion Herron had been in.

As he approached the building, the operatives who'd escorted him – minus the unconscious idiot, who'd been hauled back aboard the helicopter – peeled off and took up defensive positions. True to Zoe's word, the team who'd cornered Kearns exited the shack to form the same perimeter, leaving her alone inside. Herron wasted no time lingering. As he stepped inside and saw her on the sofa, he could see from her crestfallen look that she knew their happiness was dead. The bang of the door closing behind him was like the last nail in its coffin.

"They're pulling you back in, aren't they?" she asked, rising from her seat and moving in closer to him.

"I need to go after Shade," he replied. "He's fled to China, and—"

"And you want to finish it." There was a mix of hurt

and accusation in her voice. "Wipe out the CCP... Kill Shade..."

"Yes."

"And probably get yourself killed, too."

"You don't know that." Herron stepped forward, arms wide to embrace her. "I can take him down."

She jabbed her index finger into his chest. "And you don't know that."

"I need to do this. For myself and for us."

Realization dawned behind her eyes. "You'd go anyway, wouldn't you? Even if they hadn't threatened me."

"This is a path I need to walk."

She took a long time to respond. "I've only just found you. I don't want to lose you again."

"You won't," he said, enveloping her in his arms. "I love you, Erica."

With that, he turned and left the shack, knowing that if he delayed any longer, he might not be able to leave at all.

2

"How do I look?" Herron asked, ignoring the persistent itch from his fake beard.

"Dressed for success... Finally!" Zoe replied, her eyes on the screen of her laptop.

For the last few hours, they'd been experimenting with disguises to see which could spoof facial recognition systems, using readings from eight cameras pointed at Herron from a variety of angles. This was the tenth configuration of a wig, fake facial hair, glasses, and clothing they'd tried, and although they couldn't guarantee it would work, they had run it through at least a dozen different systems successfully. Now they had to hope it would defeat Shade's network of cell phone cameras as well.

It was just one piece of planning for an operation with a million moving parts – and even if they nailed all the preparation, once Herron was on the ground it could still all go to shit. He knew that from bitter experience.

Since leaving the shack, he'd traveled across the

country in a British private jet to a small airfield in San Diego. From there, he'd boarded a plane to Hawaii, then to the Philippines, right on the doorstep of China. Traveling in a convoy with Zoe and several of her operators, he'd been taken to a safehouse, extreme effort going into mission security the whole time. At all costs, they had to prevent him from being snapped on a cell phone.

Since then, he'd spent every waking minute preparing for the mission, which boiled down to three simple steps: infiltrate China without being detected; locate and kill Shade; secure his technology for the British Government. By denying the tech to the Chinese government, Herron would also help the millions of ordinary citizens protesting and rioting across the country. It would be his final contribution to kneecapping a regime that had caused untold misery at home and abroad, hopefully bringing about a new dawn for a fifth of the world's population.

But the odds were heavily stacked against him. The Chinese regime enjoyed significant heft – a large military, a law enforcement and intelligence apparatus aimed at maintaining the status quo and crushing any threat, and a compliant populace. But now they had their backs against the wall, and Chinese security forces would love to welcome the man who'd done so much to put them on the back foot.

If he was captured, he was a dead man.

"We done?" Herron asked, raising an eyebrow. The fake glasses on his face shifted slightly as he did.

"Almost. Take all that shit off, because it's time for you to face justice."

Herron laughed, glad to finally be able to lose the

hat, the glasses, the wig, and the fake beard. When he was done, he changed back into street gear, purchased by Zoe's people after he'd left the shack with nothing but the clothes on his back.

The safehouse was a small, three-bedroom place loaded with all the gear they needed. One room had been kitted out for a very specific purpose, with a chair, a table, a pair of handcuffs, and a high-quality digital camera on a tripod. Without waiting to be prompted, Herron sat and cuffed his wrist to the metal O-ring on the table.

"Time to be a star," Zoe said, taking up her position behind the camera. "Smile."

Herron did nothing of the sort, instead doing his best to look miserable – just like he'd been subjected to days of questioning by a foreign power. It was a look he knew well, because it was a situation he'd been in for real.

For five minutes, Zoe snapped a bunch of photographs, looking for the perfect one to use in the second element of their plan: faking Herron's arrest.

"That will do," she said, stepping away from the camera and pulling her phone from her pocket. "And we've got the report ready for the news services." She read off the phone screen. "British police have arrested wanted terrorist Mitch Herron at a street address in London. In line with the UK's international obligations, Mr. Herron will be detained until his possible repatriation to any number of the countries in which he is charged with serious crimes."

"Short and sweet," Herron said, happy enough with the wording of his fake arrest. "That's going to get some phone calls coming your way..."

"And we'll bat them away until your mission is completed. Then we'll make up some story about your escape through some nefarious scheme or other."

The ruse completed, Herron uncuffed himself. Then, after putting on his disguise again, he followed Zoe outside, breathing fresh air for the first time in days. Three SUVs with tinted windows waited for him, carrying the six plainclothes operatives who'd guarded Herron and Zoe for their entire journey from the US.

Herron didn't see any weapons, but he doubted they'd be far away. Working through all possible scenarios for such a dangerous, high-pressure mission on foreign soil, he'd filled some bags of his own with all manner of guns, blades, disguises, body armor, supplies, and other support gear. Each item had been carefully shrink-wrapped in plastic to keep it watertight, then loaded into the vehicles, ready for the journey ahead.

Herron climbed into the back seat of the second car in the convoy. Nobody joined him: the only other person in the vehicle was the driver, someone he hadn't met until now. He didn't reply to Herron's polite greeting, nor did he say anything else on the drive. That left Herron alone with his thoughts. Now, with his mission planned, he found it hard to focus on anything or anyone but Kearns. Leaving her behind had torn a hole in his heart – his soul – that he'd never felt before, and that longing was competing with the total focus his mission demanded.

He knew others who'd been distracted like this in the past: special forces soldiers or contract assassins who'd found love and ended up dead because of it.

Their business was a harsh mistress, with no place for another lover.

Yet Herron was trying anyway.

Their little convoy arrived at a small private yacht club, the sort of place where members' boats bobbed quietly in the water for most of the year before coming alive with swarms of individuals in the warmer months. It was near midnight now, though, and Herron couldn't see a single person around the clubhouse or on the pier that led to the boats. The first stage of their journey to China would go completely unobserved; even with the disguise he was wearing, Zoe's people wanted to reduce the chance of a stray cell phone camera ruining their meticulous planning.

When the operatives had secured the perimeter and given the signal Herron had been waiting for – a simple thumbs-up from the team leader – he emerged from the car and headed straight for the pier with determined strides. Zoe fell in beside him, neither of them speaking.

As he got closer, he checked out the yacht they'd provided for him. Moored under pale security lighting, it was a small vessel, like the one aboard which Herron had spent a year sailing the Pacific following the eradication of the Enclave. Designed for a crew of one, its sleek, modern design featured white fiberglass with navy blue stripes along the sides and a narrow, pointed hull that looked like it could slice through the water with ease.

It would do just fine.

Stopping beside the vessel, he turned to Zoe. "Look, I know we've had our issues, and I know what you feel for me... I just wanted to thank you for helping me so many times in the past few months. I'll get the job done."

"You're speaking like this is the last time we'll see each other," Zoe answered. "I've invested a lot of time in the success of this mission, Mitch. I expect you to do more than just get shot or captured."

"I'm being realistic. It doesn't matter how well I've prepared, I'll be alone out there. The slightest mistake and I'm dead."

"How's that any different from every other mission you've ever undertaken? And who said anything about you being alone?"

While Herron was processing this, she stepped aboard the boat.

"Wait," he said. "This wasn't part of the plan."

"Plans change."

"But you don't have a disguise."

"Yes, I do," she grinned.

"I—"

She held up a hand, cutting him short. "It's done, Mitch. I'm not going to let you fly solo on this one after your betrayal in New York. Those are the terms. Accept them or I'll have one of my guys shoot you and dump your body."

"You'd do away with me just like that? I thought you felt—"

"You've made it perfectly clear what you think about my feelings. This is business."

Herron thought about saying more, but let it go. The change of plan was frustrating, but it didn't materially change the mission. And begrudgingly or not, he had to admit Zoe was one hell of a field agent.

"Good to be working with you," she said, realizing there'd be no more resistance. "I'm taking the bed."

Herron snorted and boarded the vessel. The bright, airy interior of the cabin surprised him. To the left was a small galley with a compact sink, a two-burner stove, and a small refrigerator. The countertop was made of light-colored wood, and there were cabinets overhead for storage. Opposite was a dining area made up of a round table and two cushioned seats.

Towards the bow, he found a compact but well-designed bathroom with a toilet, a small sink, and a showerhead that could be pulled out from the wall. A sleeping area, with a double bed tucked into the corner and cabinetry made of the same light-colored wood as the galley, rounded out the amenities.

Seeing it all triggered a pang of regret about the loss of his own yacht and the simpler times he'd spent aboard it.

He shifted his mind back to business. Whatever Zoe's other strengths, as far as he knew, she didn't have any skill as a sailor, so they were relying on his experience at the helm. First, he checked the fuel levels to make sure they were adequate for the trip. Satisfied with what he found, he moved along the boat and untied the lines that secured it to the dock, careful not to let them snap too quickly and damage the hull. When the boat was floating free, he started the engine, then checked the instruments to ensure everything was working properly.

Then, finally, Herron eased the yacht out of the marina and got them underway.

* * *

IT OFTEN HAPPENED on the night before a mission – sleep evaded Herron. In the time since they'd set out from the Philippines for Shanghai, Herron had been unable to shake off the heavy cloak of doom that had settled on his shoulders.

"It's different this time, isn't it?" Zoe asked, coming up behind him. She'd turned in for the night an hour or so back, and had come up on deck in only thin cotton pajama shorts and a tank top that did nothing to ward off the chilly sea air. "Every other mission you've ever done, you could focus on it completely. Now you're split in two."

"You're a mind reader now?"

"No, just bitter experience. I've seen operatives and analysts lose their edge because they started to care about someone else. I'm seeing it again now."

"You don't need to worry about me," Herron said, then turned to grip the side rail, peering out into the vast, dark ocean. "You should get some sleep."

"Too much on my mind," she said, moving in closer to his back. "The mission... the risk... you..."

"Zoe..." Herron said, a gentle warning that failed to stop her from reaching around to put her hand on his chest. "You know that can't happen again."

"You keep thinking about how she's not here right now," Zoe said, caressing his chest and pressing her lithe figure into his back. "When you should be thankful she's not here right now..."

In any other moment of his life, Herron might have taken her up on the offer. Turned, engulfed her in his arms, kissed her passionately, letting their hands and their imaginations roam until the flame of their desire dimmed. There'd be no consequences, his mind able to separate business from pleasure, as he'd done so many times before.

But this time was different.

He stood there for a second or two, her intentions as stark as a bullet to the head. Then he reached up, gripped her hand, and gently moved it away from him. "This isn't going to happen."

"Look, I've given up on anything more than a little fun with you, Mitch," she said as she drew back, a note of irritation in her voice. "I didn't think you'd become a *total* boy scout..."

"It's a new look I'm trying on." He grinned, trying to disarm the situation. "I'm flattered, honestly, but we're sailing into the most dangerous situation either of us has ever faced. I need a clear head, and that means keeping our clothes on, if it's all the same to you."

She sighed, then nodded, and stood beside him at the rail. They stayed there for an hour or so, the boat quietly motoring towards their destiny. At last, off in the distance they spotted the bright lights of Shanghai Harbor, and Herron headed for the wheel. Zoe joined him, both watching as one of the Earth's great metropolises came into clearer view.

The closer they got, the more obvious it was the city was in trouble.

Shanghai was ablaze.

First, the fires became visible among the dark smoke obscuring the lights from the buildings. Closer in, they could spot the strobe of emergency vehicle lights, painting the city as some sort of manic disco, taken over by chaos and carnage.

It had to be the protests, the commercial heart of China brought to a standstill by riots. The Chinese leadership and their law enforcement arms would be struggling to bring a previously compliant population to heel: they'd have tried cracking the heads of a few of the more vocal and prominent protesters, then imposed a curfew, and now a lockdown, but it looked like all their measures had failed. Now millions of people would have taken to the streets, despite the threat of violence.

There was truth in the adage that when a totalitarian regime fell it fell *hard*.

"You know, you're responsible for a fair bit of that," Zoe said.

Herron shrugged. "The regime is responsible for all of it. They squeeze their people hard, so it's no surprise people look to fight back when they get a good chance. I just gave them a little push."

"Well, time to give them one more helping hand."

As if on cue, the radio crackled, emitting a voice first speaking in Mandarin, then in English. "Be aware that port entry into Shanghai by air or sea is currently restricted. Please remain offshore or otherwise depart. Any attempt to dock and enter the city will result in your arrest and the impounding of your vessel. This notice by order of the People's Liberation Army supersedes all visas and commercial permits."

"Nothing like a warm welcome," Herron said, easing back on the throttle until the boat had stopped, then killing the engine entirely. "I'll drop anchor here."

Zoe nodded and left him to it, heading below to prepare their gear for departure. Herron headed for the back of the boat, where he picked up a dozen large bottles of kerosene in a crate. Moving along the boat, he poured out bottle after bottle, dousing much of the cabin and deck.

"This thing's going to burn as bright as some of those fires in the city," Herron said as Zoe emerged, already in her wetsuit. "Shame to waste a good boat."

"Won't be a waste," she said as she readied their diving gear. "It got us to China, and burning it will protect our identity. It was *your* choice to waste the chance to create some... lasting memories."

Herron ignored the barb and focused instead on getting into his underwater gear – wetsuit, mask, fins, and the air tank rigged to his buoyancy vest. When his kit was ready, Zoe checked his kit, and he checked hers in return. Finally, he strapped a knife to one thigh and a holstered silenced pistol to the other. It was minimal armament but enough to handle anything they'd find when they first reached shore.

"Time to see how these things handle," Herron said, pulling the heavy waterproof covers from two small vehicles stowed on the stern. "Long way to swim if they crap out."

Each mini-sub looked like a small torpedo: long and cylindrical, pointed at the front, and with a small propeller at the back. The main differences, however, were that they had grab handles on the side and a storage compartment, in which Herron and Zoe had already stashed their bags of gear – guns, ammo, night vision gear, a small palm-sized device that could spoof electronic locks, a portable comms jammer, their own comms gear, a few matchbox-sized breaching charges, and all other manner of useful kit. The mini-subs were standard British kit, designed to get special operations soldiers safely to shore after disembarking from a boat or submarine and traveling underwater.

"Ladies first," Herron said. "I'll pass these down to you."

Herron waited while Zoe checked her air and entered the water, then he hefted the two torpedoes overboard. They floated well, so Zoe had no trouble corralling and securing them, ready for Herron to dive in as well.

He had one last thing to take care of.

Picking up the Zippo lighter he'd left on the deck, he sparked a flame and tossed it underarm toward the open cabin door. He didn't see it hit the deck, but there was an immediate glow of flame, which told him the kerosene had caught fire. Within seconds, he could see the fire had built and was spreading along the accelerant he'd splashed around the yacht. Satisfied, he checked his air and mask, perched on the side rail, and rolled backward overboard.

He landed in the water with a heavy splash, then swam the few short yards to where Zoe was shepherding their transports. Without speaking, he took control of one of them and pressed the button to start the engine. It started to vibrate quietly as its motor got to work, underpowered but stealthy as hell. They wouldn't get to shore fast, but Herron was pretty sure they'd get there undetected.

With one last thumbs-up to Zoe, Herron gripped the device's handles and steered it under the water, leaving the burning boat behind. He descended swiftly, confident Zoe would be right on his six, but didn't go very deep – just enough to be invisible to anyone looking out over the water, and to allow them to pass beneath any smaller boats they encountered on the way.

Although few people at MI6 knew about their operation and the Chinese authorities were being kept busy trying to suppress the uprising on the mainland, Herron spent the whole ride hoping that they wouldn't find a detachment from the Ministry of State Security waiting for them on the shore, ready to gun them down. The greatest moment of risk would be the moment they made landfall.

When they did, an hour later, it was without incident. Herron emerged from the water at a carefully selected spot in a quiet corner of the Port of Shanghai, a gargantuan facility that handled half a billion tons of container cargo a year. The scale of the port was such that it was impossible to police fully, besides which Zoe's people had found a chink in its armour.

Hacking into the network of security cameras that acted as the port's first line of defence, all the British hackers needed to do was disable three cameras at precisely the right time to give the infiltrators a clear path out and into the city, where they would meet their contact. There were still foot patrols to deal with, but drone and satellite imagery had confirmed those were few and far between... and that they were hard to miss, carrying flashlights and wearing hi-vis vests.

As Herron removed his mask and started to strip out of his gear, he turned to look at Zoe, giving her a quick smile. "Into the lair of the dragon..."

3
___

"They're pissed off, that's for sure," Herron said as they passed another set of protesters clashing with police. He kept his voice low enough for only Zoe to hear, even though few people would be paying attention to them.

"Thanks to you," Zoe murmured. "You've done more for the emancipation of the average Chinese citizen than anyone else alive."

Herron brushed off the suggestion, but he was quietly proud of the small role he'd played in helping a billion people revolt against the regime that had oppressed them for almost a century. From Fiji to the Philippines, to Hong Kong and Taiwan, he'd chipped away at the regime's authority, muddying up their plans. Then, finally, he'd helped take down the Great Firewall of China and removed the veil from the eyes of the people.

After an hour of walking through Shanghai, Herron could see the winds of change were blowing strong. Large and small protests were scattered every few blocks, with the authorities struggling to keep the people at bay. There was petty crime everywhere: theft, looting, and vandalism, all signs of a populace who'd been tightly controlled for decades finally breaking free. One of the largest cities in the world rested on a knife's edge.

Herron wondered if the situation was the same throughout China – in the dozens of metropolises housing hundreds of millions of people, or in the vast countryside where too many peasants still lived in poverty. He had to hope so, because that would be a harbinger of change more significant than Herron could dare hope for. Time would tell.

For now, his focus was on Shanghai, Shade, and the technology he'd promised to procure for the British Government.

After coming ashore, they'd changed into the street clothes they'd stowed in their bags and put on the makeup and fake facial hair that would disguise them as wealthy expatriates from any given Western country: a common enough sight in Shanghai. Leaving their duffel bags of weaponry and other gear hidden near the dock, because the first part of their mission required discretion rather than fireworks, they'd set off...

... and soon came across the first checkpoint that left Herron wishing they *had* brought the guns.

Three armored personnel carriers. A dozen heavily armed troops. A whole lot of trouble.

The troops were covering the entire intersection, checking everyone and everything seeking to move from the port to the heart of the city. Herron had known he'd have to cross paths with the authorities eventually, but he'd hoped to get a little further into the job before then.

He slowed down and turned to Zoe. "Call your people. We need to know if this is something we can detour around or if we need to go through."

As she pulled out her cell phone, Herron kept an eye on the troops. They were young guys, focused on what was immediately in front of them – the cars and people trying to get through the checkpoint – and they'd settled into a predictable routine and rhythm. Even so, he had no doubt any one of them would take the rifle on their shoulder and start shooting if a threat emerged.

"We're good," Zoe said a moment later. "My people are going to direct us past the checkpoint via parking garages and back streets."

Herron nodded, a little uncomfortable to be relying so much on the British Government, but thankful for their resources all the same. He'd been working solo since he'd left the Enclave, fighting China as a one-man band, and he wasn't going to turn down the help.

Seconds later, they were off the main street and out of sight of the checkpoints, weaving their way through back alleys. Every now and then, Zoe would pull him up, then spend a second or two checking the updated directions from her team. The whole time, Herron had no reason to think there were any flaws in the process, the satellites working to spot Chinese checkpoints and a path through them.

They walked for another fifteen minutes, getting ever closer to their objective, before Herron's mental alarm bells went off.

He heard a man's laughter.

Then a woman's scream.

Then a rifle shot.

Shanghai was a busy city, buzzing with color and movement and noise twenty-four hours a day, but it was still a city where hearing a gunshot was a big deal. The crack reverberated through the night, and Herron jogged in the direction from which he thought the sound had come, looking left and right down each alley he passed. After what felt like the millionth of them, Herron located the source: two armed soldiers, one frightened woman, and the man she'd been with lying dead on the ground, a pool of blood soaking the concrete.

Seeing red, Herron started forward, but Zoe tugged on his sleeve, pulling him back. He hissed at her. "What?"

"We should keep going," she whispered.

Herron shrugged off her grip. "She needs our help."

"Keep your eyes on the prize."

Ignoring her, he surged forward. By now, one of PRC soldiers had unbuckled his pants and was starting to lower them, looming over the frightened, half-naked girl like a terrifying spectre. The other soldier was technically meant to be standing guard, but was too busy sizing up the woman for when his turn came.

There was nothing subtle about Herron's first action. He approached in a few long strides, clearing his throat loudly. The girl cried out in Mandarin, and the man who was a second away from raping her turned to look at the new arrival. The soldier who was supposed to be on guard pivoted and raised his weapon...

Herron delivered a quick, powerful punch to the man's nose, took the rifle from him, then finished the job by smashing the crown of his skull into the soldier's face.

"Get away from her," Herron snarled at the would-be rapist as his friend dropped to the ground. "Now."

The soldier raised his hands slowly, lust replaced by fear. "No problem," he said in halting English. "You have her."

Herron fired without thinking, the simple squeeze of a trigger extinguishing the man's life. As the dead soldier fell, Herron's mind processed his loss of control, concluding in a split-second that it wasn't experience or training that had made him kill the man.

The simple fact was that he'd wanted to. And the only reason for that was Erica Kearns.

He now knew what it was like to have someone you loved threatened by murderers and monster. The poor bastard the soldiers had killed had been unable to protect the person he cared for, and throughout history in most of the world, the soldiers would have got away with it. But, in most cases and places, a man like Herron hadn't been a few feet away.

"What a fucking mess," Zoe said, her disappointment clear in her voice. "Our operational security is shot to hell."

"I couldn't let them rape her."

"You realise you've probably signed her death warrant?" Zoe replied. "Things are different here."

"Maybe not now. There's enough shouts, smoke and fire to tell me things are changing."

"We'll see if – look out!"

Herron turned like a flash to see what had prompted the warning. Two Shanghai police officers had turned the corner and were charging at him, batons drawn.

He cursed – he couldn't shoot these men. Killing or maiming soldiers who were in the process of raping a woman was one thing, but he wouldn't end the lives of cops doing their job, no matter who they worked for.

Herron ejected the magazine from the rifle and kicked it behind him, so neither of the cops could take the weapon from him and start shooting. Then he did the thing the cops would be expecting least: he counter-charged them.

Seeing the large American barreling down on them, the cops hesitated before raising their batons to defend themselves. As soon as he was in range, Herron swung his rifle like a club, the weapon smashing into one of the cop's arms and shattering his ulna. The cop shrieked and dropped his baton before staggering back and reaching up with his good hand to cradle his busted arm. For now, at least, he was out of the fight.

Still moving, Herron used the momentum of his swing to feign a blow to the other cop's knee. Instinctively, the policeman backed away, although he still managed to take a shot at his attacker. Both blows landed: Herron's rifle barely tapped his target on the leg, while the baton thumped into Herron's shoulder – painful but not enough to take him out.

The cop retreated, forced to reassess what he'd thought was a clear numerical superiority, but Herron didn't relent. Gripping the rifle lengthways with both hands, he used the ends of the weapon to deliver short, sharp, powerful blows – one end hit the cop in the cheek, the other in the chest.

The officer staggered backward. Desperate and on the defensive, he tried a few times to counter the relentless assault with swings of his baton. The first time, Herron batted the weapon away; the second, he ducked under the swing. Finally, he let go of the rifle and seized the baton in a vice-like grip. His muscles straining as the cop pulled back against him, Herron fought and won, snatching the stick away.

By now, the cop with the broken arm was reaching up to activate his radio and summon reinforcements. As he started talking in Mandarin, Herron hefted the baton to test its weight, then threw it. The club turned end over end until it smashed into the forehead of the officer, who stumbled backward and collapsed.

"You're making a grave mistake," said the cop who was still standing, his English better than the rapist Herron had just executed. "Those two soldiers are connected to the Party."

"So?"

"So, you're picking a fight with the most powerful force in China, all to save the virtue of some filthy protester who doesn't realize how this country runs."

"How this country ran," Herron said, before landing a punch in the cop's face. As the lawman dropped, Herron followed up with a kick, putting him down. "Asshole."

After taking a second to review his handiwork, Herron turned back to Zoe and awaited further censure. He was pleasantly surprised when she didn't protest; instead, she pulled out her cell phone and used Google Translate to ask the woman if she was okay.

As Zoe asked if she had somewhere to go – and if she could keep quiet about their presence here – Herron gathered up the woman's clothing and handed it to her, keeping his eyes on the goons who'd tried to hurt her. None of them were moving, and they stayed that way all the time the woman dressed.

Only when Zoe was satisfied the woman was able to leave safely and under her own power did Herron take the time to wipe his prints off the gun he'd touched and deliver one last sharp kick to the head of the wounded soldier. He didn't want the guy waking up any time soon.

"Time to go," Herron said at last. "Eyes on the prize, right?"

Her eyes flared at his mocking tone, but Zoe's pragmatism overrode her anger; they needed to get to their rendezvous. She stared at him for a while, sighed, then continued leading them on their merry way through the back streets. Block after block, they hurried on, Herron always alert for more trouble, but Zoe's contacts continued to feed directions into her ear that got them through the ring of checkpoints.

A city could never be fully buttoned up.

When they emerged onto the main streets again, they found things beyond the cordon were still under the control of the authorities. There were still cops and troops everywhere, with no hint of protests or petty crime. Businesses weren't shuttered, cars weren't burning, and people weren't walking in great mobs. It was almost as if nothing was happening elsewhere in China or in Shanghai itself; the ring of cops protected everything inside it.

While the state's forces were all over the place, Herron noticed they didn't even look twice at him or Zoe. It seemed anyone who'd passed through the checkpoints and into the center of the city was immune to scrutiny. To his mind, that kind of thinking was the bane of an authoritarian government's existence: everyone assumed someone else had done the security check and was too afraid of the consequences of speaking up.

The cynic in him also wondered if this part of the city was where the local party leaders lived and had commercial interests, the elites deploying their goons to keep their own hides safe. It didn't matter. If the protests kept up their fury, no number of batons or riot shields or firearms would stop those seeking their freedom. And, even if they didn't, those inside the ring were still screwed.

Because now Herron was in there with them, and he was hunting.

* * *

THE NIGHTSPOT where Herron and Zoe were due to meet their contact was, he'd been told, one of the hottest clubs in Shanghai. From across the street, the place looked like a bunker, all concrete walls and devoid of windows, yet no bunkers Herron had ever seen had been bathed in red strobe lights and projections of people dancing. They certainly hadn't had a line around the block to get in.

"Looks calm enough," Herron said.

Zoe nodded. "It's a Party-run establishment for the rich, famous, and connected. There wouldn't be any trouble here."

"Not yet," Herron replied. "If the PRC leadership doesn't loosen some of the screws a little, and the protesters have their way, the whole city will burn."

"Sure. But not today."

"Think that's why the contact insisted on meeting us here? Guaranteed quiet?"

"Hell if I know. But she knows where Shade is, so in we go."

And with that, she crossed the street and joined the back of the queue.

4

Two hours later, they finally made it inside the club, and as Herron walked past security, Zoe on his six, the assault on his senses was more disorienting than some war zones he'd been in. A wall of sound hit him, heavy bass like his whole body was being punched, interspersed with the high-pitched squeal of electronic music that bored deep into his brain.

It caused him to pull up short for a second. And it made him feel old.

"Never thought a little music would stop the great Mitch Herron in his tracks," Zoe shouted into his ear. "Time to party!"

The club was pulsing with energy as the heavy beats reverberated through the air, its patrons thrashing and writhing along with the music. Shafts of colorful light moved in random patterns across the enormous dance floor, painting the crowd in different hues, and Herron found himself sucked in by the sight. It felt like the club's clientele was locked into a seductive spell, the atmosphere electric.

It felt like anticipation and freedom, like the mood of the protestors not even a mile away was being manifested in a different way.

As he headed deeper into the club, searching for the bar, he marveled that the authorities hadn't yet shut this place down, given the clampdowns elsewhere. But as Zoe had said, this was a place for the rich, the famous, and the connected – he figured some Party official or another owned the place.

He fought his way through the crowd, swathed in the smells of sweat and perfume and alcohol, and finally reached the bar. More than a dozen bartenders worked at skillfully crafting cocktails, their hands blurs of motion. As someone whose reflexes and focus had kept him alive for years, Herron could appreciate their ability... but he was more interested in their faces.

It took him a minute to find the bartender whose face he had memorized from the mission briefings: a woman in the process of making what looked to be a hell of a martini – gin, shaken, not stirred. This was the woman who'd lead them to Shade, but he wasn't yet sure it was safe to make contact. So, while Zoe kept watch on him, he kept watch on the bartender, noting her manner and who she interacted with.

He kept that up for several minutes, during which time she made several cocktails and even flirted with one of her patrons, but nothing tripped any of Herron's mental alarms. At last, with a nod at Zoe, he found himself a spot at the bar and pressed a little button built into the polished stone counter: a gimmick that flashed a spotlight onto him and his seat, signaling to the staff he wanted a drink.

One of the bar staff – the *wrong* one – approached and asked him in English, "What can I get you?"

"Her," Herron said, gesturing with his chin at the woman he'd been tasked with meeting.

The bartender frowned and looked like he might take issue with the request, until Herron put a stack of yuan notes on the bar. It wasn't a huge amount of money for a bartender at a posh club, but it was easy money. The note was gone a moment later, its new owner on his way to fetch Herron's contact.

The woman sauntered over, a cocktail shaker still in her hand, then leaned on the bar with her elbows.

"You want my tits or my ass?" The woman asked. "No other reason to ask for me specifically."

"Neither, actually. I want a special drink for my British friend over there..."

The woman's expression gave away no clues. "Gordon's?"

"Bombay Sapphire," Herron said, completing the codeword exchange.

"Only the finest for His Majesty's finest." She pointed to a roped-off section, the only sparsely populated area of the club. "Head over there, and I'll bring it right over."

Whereas the entire bar and dance floor area was pulsating with an immense crowd, the section he'd been directed to only had a small number of well-dressed, bored-looking people sprinkled through the tables. Controlling access to the area, standing next to the rope, was a thick-set man in a suit; despite the expensive tailoring, it still showed the bulge of a weapon under his armpit.

Herron approached cautiously, not taking his eye off the goon. He trusted Zoe was behind him and that the plan she'd figured out with the bartender to get hold of Shade's location was sound... and sure enough, as he got closer to the rope, the security man did nothing to stop him. Apparently, subliminal awareness of those the bar staff had directed to the VIP area was part of the job description.

He took a seat with Zoe at one of the small circular tables, a single burning candle the only thing atop it, and shared a slight nod before settling in to wait.

Minutes passed, then an hour, the music in the club continuing to pound and its patrons continuing to enjoy themselves like nothing at all was happening outside. The whole time, Herron didn't so much as glance at the bartender; despite their success crossing into China and then getting inside the Party's security cordon, as westerners, he and Zoe still stuck out here, and there was every chance they were being watched.

"How much longer is she going to be?" Herron yelled into Zoe's ear. "We're exposed here."

"We're fine. We'll get Shade's location, go back to where we left the guns, arm up, then get after him."

Herron had his doubts, but he kept quiet because he didn't have a better plan. Cooling their heels here wasn't what he'd had in mind when—

"Herron!" Zoe's scream was loud enough to be heard over the pounding music, a visceral shriek that had none of the professionalism of a career spy. She was clutching her side, blood spewing through her fingers and her eyes wide with shock.

Bursting from his seat, and wishing again they'd brought the guns with them, he seized Zoe and lowered her to the ground, making them harder targets. The noise from the sound system had masked the shot, and he had no idea where it had come from – this was the best he could do to avoid another while he swiftly assessed her wound.

Judging by the amount of blood Zoe was losing, she was in a hell of a lot of trouble.

"Where?" Herron said, coiling to move, his mind shifting from first aid to threat analysis. "Zoe! Where?"

She coughed, but it was clear she was in shock, unable to process the question. Herron scanned the dance floor. The goon guarding the VIP area was still in place, none the wiser that one of the clients behind him had been shot. Continuing to sweep the crowd, Herron searched for anyone who *wasn't* dancing. Just as his eyes passed over the bar area, he spotted the woman he'd been waiting to serve them – the MI6 contact – raising a gun.

She opened fire...

...and blew out the brains of a man standing nearby, his own weapon up to finish off Herron.

The bartender caught his eye, and they nodded at each other. Whoever she was, she was now Herron's best bet to get Zoe out alive. While the first shooting had gone unnoticed, there was no way the crowd around the bar could miss the second. Immediately, the clubbers surged like a single creature, fleeing the scene. Her pistol up and ready, the bartender pushed through them, heading towards the VIP area.

"Come on," Herron yelled at Zoe, wrapping one of her arms over his shoulder and doing his best to support her weight. "Press on the wound with your other hand."

Still holding up his partner, Herron jabbed a finger past the bartender, pointing over her shoulder. The woman spun, raised her pistol at the two armed, uniformed soldiers advancing on them with murderous intent in their eyes.

She fired twice, dropping both men like their strings had been cut.

"You're popular!" she shouted at Herron. "You think the authorities have figured out who you are?"

"I met a few of their friends a couple of hours ago," Herron bellowed. "I'm surprised it took them this long to find me. Is there a back way out of here?"

The woman cupped her hand up to her ear, then decided on a new strategy. Pirouetting to face the DJ booth, she aimed the gun up at the man behind the decks and made a 'cut it' signal across her throat with her hand. Herron saw the DJ's eyes widen in alarm, then suddenly, abruptly, the music stopped.

"That's better," the bartender said. "What was the question?"

"Back exit?" Herron repeated.

"Sure." She gestured with her chin toward a door. "But that's where they keep the garrison."

Herron gave her a flat look. "You station troops in your *nightclubs*?"

"It's China. You need to make sure there's no soldiers in the bathroom before you go..."

"Whatever. Let's go..." Herron stopped mid-sentence. He had no idea of her name.

"Call me Sapphire." She smirked. "As in Bombay Sapphire."

"Cute," Herron snorted, then steadied Zoe on his shoulder. "We need to move before—"

As if on cue, four soldiers burst through the exit door and raced toward them.

"I've got this," Sapphire said, and before Herron could react, she burst into a run toward the armed men, sliding behind the cover of a floor-to-ceiling stone pillar.

He wasn't sure what she was planning, but there was no way out until she cleared the path. Seizing the chance to attend to Zoe's wound, he laid her down and got to work, trying to staunch the bleeding.

Immediately recognizing Sapphire as a threat, the soldiers opened fire, peppering the stone column with rounds. If the earlier gunplay hadn't cleared the dancefloor, there'd be civilians dropping like flies.

As it was, Sapphire was pinned down.

The PRC soldiers advanced, their sinister intent unmistakable. Herron's heart raced, adrenaline flooding his body, but all his efforts were focused on keeping Zoe alive. Without a weapon of his own, it was the best he could do.

For a moment, the clatter of gunfire stopped, all four men pausing to reload... then Sapphire emerged in her full glory, moving swiftly, pistol held with confidence.

She moved from the pillar to the cover of an upturned steel table, shooting as she ran. Her shots were considered and precise. One soldier dropped, drilled between the eyes, then another, earning himself a gut shot. By now, the remaining pair had reloaded and started blazing away again as Sapphire made it to cover.

Herron assessed the room. In coming after

Sapphire, the soldiers had left the way clear to the exit. "Time to go," he said, hauling Zoe to her feet again.

Bullets whizzed past him, shattering walls and furniture, but he had to get Zoe to the help she needed. Ahead of him, Sapphire was trapped in cover again, waiting for her next move. Her face was fierce, focused. Resolute.

It was as if the chaos around her fueled her determination.

It was a feeling Herron knew well.

The soldiers continued unloading at Sapphire, rather than take out the two sitting ducks inching toward them. Making it to the pillar that had sheltered Sapphire only moments ago, Herron rested Zoe against it and looked for a way to join the fight. With Sapphire still outgunned, he needed to be more than a bystander if they were to make it out of here.

He picked up two heavy glass tumblers that had been knocked off a table and yet remained unbroken. Testing their weight, he locked eyes with Sapphire; in less than a second, they'd both silently agreed on a plan.

Taking a deep breath, Herron rounded the pillar and pitched his best fastball at one of the soldiers.

He had no idea if the glass had hit or not, but it didn't matter: the soldiers responded to the new threat instantly, spinning and firing, even as Herron ducked back behind the pillar. The distraction was just what Sapphire needed. She fired once, twice, three times... and silence descended upon the shattered nightclub.

It lasted only a moment, the distant wails of approaching sirens gradually growing louder. As Herron helped Zoe to the door, Sapphire paused to put a round into the head of each of the soldiers, making sure the job was done. Then she reached down for one of their pistols and handed it to Herron.

"They're going to be coming for us in force now," she said as she reloaded. "We're going to have to run, fast."

Herron held her gaze for a second, the unspoken meaning of her words hanging heavy between them. Zoe was barely conscious, bleeding badly, and – to his practiced eye – had less than an hour before even a hospital couldn't save her.

He couldn't get her to help and still complete his mission.

"The authorities are a few minutes out..." Sapphire's voice was gentle but insistent, prodding Herron toward a decision. "I know you don't want to leave her, but they are her best shot."

But Herron wasn't about to leave Zoe at the mercy of the same government who'd once sent him to rot in China's equivalent of a gulag. "You stay and get her to safety. Just tell me where to find Shade and I'll—"

"Oh, honey, Zoe didn't tell you?" Sapphire interrupted. "That information's contingent on me coming with you to kill him."

Herron glared at her. He didn't have time for this. "Why?"

"That's my business. It's also non-negotiable. So you need to decide, because the cops will be kicking the door down in about 30 seconds."

"Fuck it," Herron growled and lowered Zoe to the ground. He looked into her eyes, which were open but glassy. "I'm sorry," he said.

Zoe blinked, then tried to speak, but her words were a largely indecipherable mumble.

Outside, the sirens were getting louder. Herron

gripped her hand. "If they take you into custody, I'll get you out."

He waited a second for her to respond, but she simply blinked again.

"Tick tock," Sapphire said over his shoulder.

Herron climbed to his feet and nodded at Sapphire to lead the way, knowing there was every chance that Zoe – a woman who'd helped him rescue Kearns and pursue Shade, regardless of their differences – may not survive the night.

But he had a job to do and only one way to do it.

The door Sapphire led him through opened on a dimly lit corridor that smelled of booze and cleaning supplies. The rear of the club nowhere near as luxurious as the public areas, a flickering light bulb adding an air of trepidation to their clandestine escape. However, as they moved swiftly past several small offices and a large common room – home, no doubt, to the garrison – no new danger confronted them.

At the exit, Sapphire used her staff pass to unlock and open the door. She stuck her head out, and once she was satisfied the coast was clear, waved to Herron to follow. The door closed behind them, leaving them surrounded by shadows and the damp embrace of the night. Outside the walls of the club, they could not only hear the scream of sirens, but also the distant rumble of military vehicles.

The authorities knew their party was over: the threat outside the cordon was now in their midst.

Thankfully, the party that had been inside the club didn't look to have quite finished yet.

Hundreds of revelers were flooding the streets, many picking up where they'd left off with their trancelike dancing, moving in time to the police sirens. Some of them would be high, some of them drunk, and others just along for the ride, but the combination gave Herron and Sapphire an easy group of civilians to blend in with. Emerging from the alleyway, they pushed right in amongst the clubbers, dancing and writhing as best they could.

It was a skill for which Sapphire had far more aptitude than Herron.

"You're awful," she smirked, getting in close to him, doing her best to hide their faces from the cops and soldiers. "Move to the edge of the dancers, and we'll get the hell out of here."

Herron didn't have to be told twice. The other revelers parting around them, Herron and Sapphire moving like fish through water until they were near enough to slip into another alley on the far side of the street. There were a few cops there, but nowhere near as many as at the front of the club.

"Wait for my mark," Sapphire said, speaking with a confidence Herron found appealing. Combined with her skills in a fight, it made him wonder who'd trained her. "Now!"

Together, they ceased dancing and broke into a run, stopping for nothing. A cop shouted after them, but they were so far away so quickly that the officer didn't bother to pursue. Presumably, he had enough to deal with managing the club and the streets outside.

Cutting through several alleys and bypassing a handful of roving police patrols, Herron and Sapphire soon made it to an empty street. They were safe.

And at Sapphire's car.

"Nice wheels," Herron said, sizing up the sporty

ride. "Not what you usually see a bartender driving around in."

"I get good tips," Sapphire smirked, climbing into the driver's seat and gunning the engine. "Now to go get Shade..."

"First, we go get my gear, *then* we go get Shade..."

She looked like she might argue, but then she shrugged. "Fine. Strap in."

5

"Got everything?" Sapphire said as Herron got back in the car and closed the door. "Ready to go?

Herron nodded, buckled his seatbelt and stashed his pistol in the glove compartment. "Pistol in there, a few tech toys in my pocket, and the heavy artillery in the trunk..."

"Sounds promising..."

Herron smirked as she put her foot to the floor and got them on the road, quickly surmising that Sapphire had been given training in pursuit driving. He'd suspected it during the time she'd spent driving him to where he and Zoe had left their guns, but now – as she zig zagged through traffic – he watched in awe. She milked every ounce of performance from a car that had plenty to give and had them on the road out of Shanghai inside of 15 minutes.

"Where are we headed?" Herron asked. "I really should stay close to Shanghai, see if I can spring Zoe from wherever they end up taking her..."

"She's dead, in the hospital with a gut shot, or in custody with a gut shot," Sapphire replied. "Whichever, she's going nowhere fast. More than I can say for Shade."

"He's on the move?"

"No, but he's got a meeting tomorrow with the Ministry of State Security. If we don't intercept him before then, he's going to hand over the facial recognition software for a truck full of cash and protection by the government."

"And then?"

"And then he's untouchable," she said, pulling out to pass a car and then cutting back in front of it and powering away. "The regime *might* fall, but I wouldn't count on it. If they get that technology, it *definitely* won't. The MSS would track, arrest and torture every protest leader they know about. That would reveal the identities of more protest leaders. Within days, the groups would start to splinter – large groups would become small groups, and small groups would become isolated individuals."

"And the uprising would die quietly," Herron murmured. "They did the same thing in Hong Kong. I tried to stop them."

"You failed." Sapphire's words stung. "They took over the island. Now everyone there's under the same brutal control as the mainland."

"Listen, I've done more to fight this regime than anyone," Herron snapped. "I'm aware of the stakes. You just get me to Shade and I'll get the job done."

Without waiting for a reply, he closed his eyes and settled in for the drive. They'd taken a short detour to pick up the gear he and Zoe had stashed, at which point

Sapphire had revealed they were headed to Beijing. The trip from Shanghai would take around 12 hours. He'd offered to split the driving, but Sapphire had insisted she take the wheel the whole time.

Might as well use the time to get some sleep.

With his eyes closed and the conversation over, Herron's mind wandered – the first opportunity he'd had to compute the broader ramifications of what had happened back at the club. With Zoe dead or captured, he could simply walk away from this, if he wanted to...

No chance.

* * *

"Herron, wake up," Sapphire said, punching him gently in the leg. "We've got company."

Herron blinked a few times, snapping back to an alert state. "How many? Where?"

"Two cars, on our ass for the last ten minutes. Make yourself useful."

Herron did just that, reaching for his weapon in the glove compartment as he kept his eyes on the passenger-side mirror. While neither he nor Sapphire could identify the drivers of the chase cars, his instincts matched hers: they were clearly a tail. And now the first of the two sedans was getting closer.

As he found his pistol and flicked off the safety, in the mirror, he saw a man lean out of the window of the lead sedan. There could be only one reason to do that.

"Gun!" Herron shouted, but Sapphire was already on it. She cut across two lanes as the chase car's passenger opened fire, the rapid flash of the submachine gun strobing in the mirror. Bullets ripped through the air, shattering the windows and punching welts into the car's fuselage; it would have been a hell of a lot worse if not for her quick thinking.

Skilfully Sapphire weaved in and out of traffic, presenting as mobile a target as possible, leaving Herron to respond to the attack. He unbuckled his seatbelt, wound down the window, and, taking a deep breath, waited for his moment.

The hail of lead ceased – the gunman was reloading. Easing himself out of the window, facing backward and whipped by the wind, Herron aimed and fired.

The submachine gun had been a full rock-and-roll maelstrom, peppering their vehicle with rounds and hitting who knew how many civilians with the strays. Herron, on the other hand, was precise and accurate, firing single shots that punctuated the chaos.

He put one, two, three rounds into the gunman's chest, causing him to slump forward, still hanging out of the window. The submachine gun slipped from his dead fingers and bounced, clattering onto the road, the reload never completed.

"One down!" Herron shouted to Sapphire, who responded by running a red to take a quick left at an intersection.

"How the hell did they get onto us?"

Herron said nothing, but he knew exactly what had brought the attention down on them: his intervention in the alleyway. That had put him and Zoe on the radar of the Chinese authorities, costing Zoe dearly and making the mission a hell of a lot harder.

"More of them..." Herron shouted as the dead gunman was dragged back inside the car and replaced by another. Meanwhile, the second sedan was getting closer, its own shooter hanging out the window. "Two shooters now!"

Herron traded shots with the pair, none of his rounds finding their mark, enemy bullets whizzing past his head or pounding into the car's bodywork. The barks of gunfire and the roaring of high-performance cars reverberated through the streets, a symphony of danger and desperation.

Out of ammo, Herron was forced back inside to reload, giving the chase cars the break they needed.

"They're closing," Sapphire said, as Herron slammed home a new magazine. A bullet from one of the enemy shooters blew through the windshield between them. "Time to change up the formula a little."

Herron had no chance to reply before Sapphire wrenched the wheel, veering them into a narrow alleyway at batshit crazy speed. The pursuing sedans followed through the maze of twists and turns, trash cans and dumpsters. Sapphire pushed the car to its limits, executing expert hairpin turns and accelerating through tight gaps, her pursuers struggling to keep up.

It confirmed to Herron that Sapphire was more than just an MI6 intel source: he was a hell of a driver, but she had him beat.

"You hit?" Herron asked, checking over her body with his eyes and his hands, because she was unable to do so herself. "I think you're good."

She nodded, distracted by the difficulty of the driving. "I can't shake them..."

"Let me try to help."

While the mad chase through the alleyways prevented the Chinese gunmen from shooting at them, it also meant Herron couldn't hang out of the window and shoot back – the corners were too tight to guarantee he wouldn't be pancaked against a wall or a dumpster. Instead, he turned, kneeling on his seat with his chest pressed against its back, and fired through the shattered rear windshield. He didn't hold back, unloading the entire clip at the nearest pursuit car – specifically at the driver. His shots pounded into the windshield, and just as the chase spilled out onto the main streets again, he finally struck a blow, nailing the man behind the wheel.

As Sapphire once again turned them onto a three-lane road, tires squealing, the lead pursuit vehicle – now driverless – plowed into a civilian car, its horn blaring constantly. Herron punched the air in elation, then got to work reloading.

Just as he was about to start shooting at the second – and final – chase car, two more appeared behind it.

"They're like a fucking hydra..." Herron muttered, as he started shooting again. "Cut off one head and more appear."

The car slewed, Sapphire fighting the wheel for control, as one of their tires blew out: in an instant, a lucky shot from their pursuers had changed the dynamic of the chase.

Sapphire cursed, but all Herron could do was focus instead on taking out another of the cars. As the vehicle directly behind them veered off the road, its driver dead, Sapphire snapped, "Grab hold of something!"

Without waiting for him to do so, she swerved into an underground parking lot – if Herron hadn't been gripping the back of his seat, he might have been thrown clear.

They were driving on the rim of the wheel now, a trail of sparks in their wake. Sapphire aimed for the ramps to the higher levels, up and up and up and up, racing along the tight avenues between parked cars on either side of them. Herron hoped no bastard wanted to come *down*, because they'd hit head-on at fatal speed.

He also wondered what the hell they were going to do when they hit the top level...

Sapphire started laughing maniacally, and he turned in his seat to look. "Oh, no..."

The last ramp, which led to the rooftop, was built very close to a neighboring building.

Sapphire floored it and – after a final burst of extreme acceleration – they hit the ramp at speed.

The car caught air, defying gravity for a heart-stopping moment, before landing with a bone-rattling crash on the adjacent rooftop. The black sedans, still on their tail, were too slow to react, unable to replicate the daring feat. They screeched to a halt at the edge of the parking lot's rooftop.

Sapphire and Herron exchanged a glance of relief and satisfaction.

"Time to go," Sapphire said, unbuckling her seatbelt and opening the door. "Follow me out this side, and keep the body of the vehicle between us and them."

Herron did so, waiting until she was clear then angling his body through the car to emerge through the driver's side door. Crouching low on the rooftop, he tossed his pistol to her. "Cover me."

Sapphire caught the gun and rose to fire, as Herron moved fast and low toward the back of the car. He waited for a break in the enemy submachine gun fire then scrambled, opening the trunk and pulling out the heavy bag of guns and other gear. It was everything he'd need to take down Shade – he couldn't leave it behind.

The whole movement only took a second, by which time the Ministry operatives were peppering his end of the vehicle again. Sapphire finished unloading her clip and then moved away, using the length of the sports car to cover them from the enemy gunfire. Herron followed, making for a fire escape. They climbed down, all the way to the ground, before sprinting for several blocks – Sapphire still holding the pistol and Herron hauling the bag of guns.

At last they were far enough away to consider themselves safe. For now.

"That was some fine driving," Herron said. "Who trained you?"

She shook her head. "A girl can't give you all her secrets on the first date, buddy. But stick around, and I'm sure there'll be more surprises as we get to know each other..."

A hint of suggestion lingered in the air, but Herron ignored it. "We'll need to get some more wheels if we're going to get to Beijing in time. Why don't you wait here while I go steal something?"

"Fat chance," she laughed. "You got four MSS cars and a dozen agents on our ass faster than you could blink. You probably lured them to the nightclub as well."

"That's Shade's technology."

"Wrong. The MSS hasn't got their hands on it yet. Don't underestimate China's own capability in locating, tracking, and killing its enemies. They've cultivated it for decades."

"Fine," Herron said. He hated the idea that taking out the soldiers and cops in the alley had got the heat on them – and cost Zoe so much. "You go get a car, then."

She nodded and left the alley, finally giving Herron a second alone to think. He leaned against the wall and slid down it onto his ass, the bag resting next to him. His head was spinning a little – this mission was supposed to start easy and only get hard when he and Zoe found Shade. Instead, it had been a nightmare from the beginning; everything that could go wrong had gone wrong.

And all the while, he longed to be back by Kearns' side. Every minute they were apart, he missed her... and there was no guarantee he'd ever see her again.

Had this maelstrom of thoughts cost him his edge? Used to working alone, he suddenly had all these other people to factor in. But it was an inescapable paradox: he had to work with Zoe to get to Sapphire, had to rely on Sapphire to get to Shade, and had to get to Shade to get home to Kearns. Everything relied on everything else, until he was face-to-face with his nemesis. Then he could pull the trigger – several times – and end the cancer that had plagued his life and the complexity his life had become.

He was still pondering this when a beat-up Toyota sedan screeched to a halt at the mouth of the alley. He waited until Sapphire wound the window down, then, sure it was her, he climbed to his feet and hauled the bag over to the car.

This time, he put it in the back seat, so the heavy artillery could be accessed easily if they picked up a tail again.

6

———

"Where are we?" Herron asked, blinking away hours of heavy sleep.

"Beijing," Sapphire said. "I was just about to wake you. We're only fifteen minutes from the apartment building Shade is holed up in. I thought you'd want a few minutes to get your stuff together."

"I'm ready," Herron said, looking out the window as shops and parked cars whizzed by. Many of them showed signs of damage from the uprising. "Looks like the protesters have been busy here."

"Makes sense. This is the seat of power. It's no surprise this is where an angry public would direct most of its attention."

"And get gunned down for their trouble," Herron muttered, as they passed a few soldiers milling about a cordoned area. There were body bags on the ground nearby. "Imagine what will happen if the government can find anyone, anywhere, instantly."

"They win. And so does Shade, because he'll have sold them everything they need to do it."

"Assuming he makes that meeting."

Herron's words lingered in the tight confines of the car as Sapphire went back to driving. He gazed absentmindedly out the window, and the fifteen minutes passed as quick as a flash. Sapphire pulled the car to a stop out front of a large apartment building and killed the engine; as if on cue, there came a boom of thunder and the first patter of rain on their windshield.

"Well, that's ominous, isn't it?" Sapphire laughed, opening the door. "Hope you're not superstitious. If you are, I'd be getting the hell out of here right now."

Herron reached over to the back seat for his bag, Sapphire put a hand on his arm, stalling him.

He frowned. "No guns?"

"Bring only your pistol and whatever tech toys you can fit in your pocket," she said. "We're going to be crossing a lobby filled with civilians; we can't be packing anything heavy."

"No other way to Shade?" Herron said. He wanted to be fully armed for this. She shook her head and he sighed. "Fine. Pistols only."

They crossed the street and entered the building. Walking side by side through the busy lobby, they headed for the elevator, Herron feeling a dozen sets of eyes on him. Several of the residents were staring a little too much; perhaps it was the presence of two westerners in a residential apartment building, but he doubted it. There were enough tourists and expats in Beijing that an American and a Brit shouldn't be too much of an oddity.

That left one possibility.

"We've been made," Herron said softly, so only Sapphire could hear.

"None of these guys are a threat," Sapphire replied. "But a few of them might try to stop us."

"Let them," Herron said, gritting his teeth with determination.

His hand hovered near the pistol in the waistband of his pants while Sapphire called the elevator. Herron kept his eyes moving, Sapphire too, but nobody watching them made a move. With a soft ping, the elevator arrived, its doors opened... and Herron was relieved to find no trouble waiting for them inside.

They both leaned against the back wall as the doors started to close. But a half-second before the doors were fully shut, a man stuck his arm into the gap, triggering the sensor that opened them again. Two Chinese stepped inside, both with hard faces, both wearing suits. They nodded at Herron and Sapphire – polite enough, but there was no warmth in their greeting. They turned to face the front and the doors started to close again.

For anyone else, they might have gotten away with portraying themselves as fellow passengers. Herron, however, noticed neither of them had bothered to press a button for a floor.

He glanced sideways at Sapphire. She gave him a slight nod. She'd also caught the fact the men hadn't selected a floor: a rookie mistake by two operatives focused on the fight to come rather than hiding their intentions.

As the elevator ascended, Herron kept his eyes locked on the pair, taking advantage of the reflective metal walls to watch them from multiple angles. So when one of them reached inside his coat – for a pistol or a blade – he was ready.

With lightning reflexes, Herron and Sapphire lunged towards their adversaries.

Knowing that firing their guns would alert everyone in the building before they'd had a chance to get to Shade, they focused on disarming the Chinese men. Herron twisted and contorted in the cramped space, elbows and knees putting in work, focusing more on putting his opponent down. His strikes were swift, calculated, powerful strikes, every movement a blur of violence. But while the flurry of blows prevented the Chinese agent from drawing his weapon, they failed to take his highly skilled opponent out of the fight.

At least until Sapphire gave him a hand. Delivering a devastating headbutt to her adversary, she sent him staggering back and into Herron's more capable foe. It was enough to give Herron the opening he needed, slamming a right hook to the jaw of the operative. One was all it took: the man dropped like a stone.

Sapphire, meanwhile, was finishing off her own opponent: a low kick buckled his leg, before an immediate knee to the head laid him out.

By the time the elevator doors opened with a soft 'ding,' both Chinese operatives were out cold.

"Nice warm-up," she said. "Get their guns while I make sure the coast is clear."

Herron dug into their jackets and pulled out two pistols. He removed their magazines and pocketed them, then tossed the guns out of the elevator and into the hall. When he was done, he pressed every button on the panel and stepped out into the hallway, sending the pacified agents on a long ride while they slept.

They walked down the hallway, Sapphire leading and Herron covering her back. They had their weapons out now, the ability to put Shade down instantly if he emerged trumping any consideration of stealth. Even then, their pistols might not be enough to see Shade off, and Herron regretted not being able to bring the heavy firepower along.

He kept his eyes moving, glancing at the number plates on the doors as he passed. The sequence of numbers was logical and predictable – even numbers on the left and odd numbers on the right. No more than thirty seconds after they'd exited the elevator, Sapphire said, "Here. 1209."

Herron gestured for Sapphire to take up a position on one side of the door while he took the other. After a quick exchange of nods, Herron tried the handle: locked. Reaching into his pocket, he pulled out the electronic lock spoofer and, ten seconds after holding it over the lock and pressing the single button on the device, it beeped and flashed green. Leading with his pistol, he entered the hallway of the small but modern apartment. All the lights were on, and soft music was playing somewhere deeper inside.

"Clear," Herron whispered as he passed the bedroom on the left, quickly scanning inside.

"Clear," Sapphire repeated from the doorway to the bathroom.

Only the conjoined kitchen, dining, and living area remained.

The large, open-plan area formed the bulk of the apartment. It was of a contemporary design: the kitchen had state-of-the-art stainless-steel appliances, complemented by gleaming granite countertops and an oversized island, while the living area was adorned with plush sofas and a minimalist entertainment center.

But for all that he *did* see as he swept the area – needless detail that his brain disregarded without a second thought – Herron *didn't* see the one thing he wanted to: Shade. At least, not until Shade popped up from behind the island bench and fired several shots his way – *pop pop pop*.

The suppressed rounds bored into the wall next to Herron's head, forcing him back.

"Game's up, Shade," Herron said, pressing his back against the wall. He was under no illusion the drywall would protect him if Shade started firing blind, but it was better than nothing.

Shade laughed. "Just how many times are you going to threaten me with your bluff and bluster, Mitch?"

"This is the last – you're cornered." He glanced at Sapphire, lowering his voice to a whisper. "He's behind cover, the kitchen island bench." She nodded.

"Sure," Shade called out, "but I can shoot my way through you, or kick your ass. In fact, I'm quite looking forward to it, Mitch. I'm glad you found me here."

"Quit stalling," Herron replied. "Back up isn't coming. We dealt with your Chinese minders on the way up here."

"We?" Shade laughed. Herron cursed silently. He hadn't intended to reveal Sapphire's presence in the apartment; now he'd wasted a potential wildcard. "And as for the MSS grunts," Shade went on, "I told them you were persistent and they'd need more firepower, but they insisted you'd never even find your way onto the mainland."

"It's over, Shade, we're here to finish this once and for all."

"I'm afraid you and your British friend are going to

be disappointed. You ooze failure, Mitch. You've become so focused on being a good little servant to whichever government strong-arms you that you've lost sight of the big picture – making tons and tons and tons of money."

Herron grinned to himself. Shade thought Sapphire was Zoe, an easy enough assumption given Herron wasn't known for having a large Rolodex of female companions. The mistake might give them back an edge.

There was only one way to find out.

Nodding at Sapphire, Herron did what he'd hoped Shade wouldn't, and fired through the drywall. The unsilenced rounds punched through the plaster, aimed at where Herron hoped Shade would be – if they didn't hit him, at least they would force Shade to duck behind cover.

After his third shots, Herron heard a cry of pain. Exploding from cover, he crossed the room.

"Got you, asshole," Herron grinned, leveling his weapon at Shade. The bullet had taken the former assassin in his gun hand. "Give me the facial recognition technology, and I'll put one in your head. Or don't, and I'll take a little longer..."

Clearly pained, Shade opened his mouth to respond... then his gaze drifted past Herron and locked onto something over his left shoulder. "Oh, you blind idiot, Herron."

"Nice try. That's the oldest trick in the book."

"Drop the piece."

Herron half-turned to see Sapphire holding two pistols – one pointed at Shade, the other at him.

Stunned, Herron dropped his weapon. "What the hell are you playing at, Sapphire?"

"The Chinese Government wants Shade's tech but doesn't want the blowback of harboring him, or the trouble of having to kill him themselves. And you were marked already."

"But they don't have the tech yet," Herron said.

"Oh, wake up," Shade mocked. "We did the deal yesterday. I'm a little hurt they've sent their little attack dog after me before the ink is even dry."

"Why wait until we were together?" Herron asked, re-focusing the conversation on Sapphire. All the time he kept her talking and not shooting, he could figure out a plan. "You could have just let the cops kill me back at the club."

She smirked. "One of you at a time is no challenge. I thought taking both of you at once I might at least work up a sweat."

"That's a big call," Herron replied.

Shade chuckled, his eyes on Sapphire. "I don't think our good friend Mitch has figured out who you are yet..."

She sneered, never taking her gaze off Herron. "Honey, I'm your worst nightmare. I taught Shade everything he knows."

"She taught *all* the Alphas everything they knew," Shade added. "She's bad fucking news. The worst of the fucking worst. And you brought her *here*."

Herron's eyes widened. The Alphas had been the Enclave's elite killers, far more skilled than Herron. He'd thought Shade was the last of them left alive, a formidable opponent who'd out-fought Herron time and again. The addition of another into the mix – one claiming to have been the instructor for all the others – changed everything.

"How did you survive the battle that wiped out the Master and the rest of the Enclave?" Herron asked. While he had to keep her talking, he was also genuinely curious. "Shade was imprisoned, what's your story?"

"I cut school."

"So why break cover now? No one's been looking for you, you've been safe –"

"I've been bored! Then, when I found out MI6 had 'arrested' the nefarious *Mitch Herron*, my spidey sense started to tingle. I made a few phone calls to some old friends in London..."

"And inserted yourself into the picture."

"Sure did. You see, those shadows you guys like to hide in?" She took a step closer to Herron and pressed her pistol against his temple. "I own them."

Herron's mind raced, frantically trying to find an out, a way to killing Shade and Sapphire, and get the technology back...

"Well then, you'd better take out Shade first," he said. "He's a crafty bastard. You can't trust him to stay where he is while you put me down, even with a bullet in his hand."

"Thanks for the advice," Sapphire said, her tone suggesting she'd give it zero consideration. "But if it's all the same to you, I'd rather just shoot you both at the same tim—"

She grunted in pain, as something metallic clanged on the tiled floor of the kitchen. A split second later, the pressure of the gun against his head eased off a little – not a sure-fire sign he'd caught a break, but the best he was going to get.

He swung an elbow back and connected with

Sapphire. As the air whooshed from her, the lights went out.

Herron scrambled for cover, using his memory of the apartment layout to move. His arms out in front of him, he felt the cold marble of the island bench and vaulted over it without a second's delay, landing around where Shade should be.

Sapphire fired blind, her bullets pounding into the furniture and the walls.

"Really, Shade?" Sapphire called out. "Throwing a pot at my head and turning out the lights?"

"You said you wanted a challenge."

"That wasn't what I had in mind."

"Well, saving Herron wasn't what I had in mind," Shade replied. "But I'm the only one who gets to kill that bastard. Now leave."

"Oh, honey, the only way you're getting rid of me is in a body bag."

As the former teacher and pupil swapped barbs, Herron was silently focusing on arming himself. He slowly and quietly slid open the top drawer on the island bench, hoping – as in every other house on the entire planet – it contained cutlery. One at a time, as quietly as she could, he withdrew several knives, testing each blade with his thumb. Eventually, he found a pair of serrated steak knives, the best he could hope for, given the circumstances.

Silently, he advanced, low and slow, to where he thought Sapphire might be, on the other side of the island bench. He had only a vague idea where Shade had relocated himself, judging from their tactically flawed exchange of banter, but his old enemy was a threat to be dealt with later.

He inched through the room, his eyes fighting the dark and his ears fighting the silence, hoping for some sign of his target. Sapphire and Shade would also be searching, their senses straining, three of the deadliest people on the planet stalking one another in the confines of a small apartment. The first to locate someone would likely get a kill, which would make enough noise for the third person to deal with them too.

Such were the brutal calculations of combat in the dark.

Herron briefly thought about retreating, but he couldn't run while the last remaining elements of the Enclave were in the room. No matter the odds, this was his chance to kill the last few people standing between him and a peaceful life on the lake with Kearns, ending his business with his corrupt former employers, his greatest foe, and the CCP.

He kept his thoughts focused on survival, on using whatever he had at his disposal to end this.

"You're both dead, you know?" Sapphire said. "As soon as I find where the damn light switch, I'm going to put a bullet in both of you..."

"Good luck with that," Shade said, from somewhere across the other side of the room. "I used a switch under the island benchtop that kills all the power – the lights, the outlets, everything..."

Herron's eyes widened in the darkness. Shade was clearly communicating a way he could hit the lights... but doing so had informed Sapphire too. Herron heard her moving in the direction of the countertop. Time was of the essence: if she reached the light switch before he did, she'd gain the initiative.

If he reached it first, without a gun of his own, the

odds would still be stacked against him. But he'd have a chance.

The only questions were Shade's motivation and his allegiance.

Herron softly laid down one of the knives and felt around the underside of the benchtop with his free hand, finding the small switch after a second or two. He clicked it.

Instantly the room lit up, revealing Sapphire three feet away on the other side of the bench – just too far for Herron to use his remaining knife.

Sapphire took a step back and aimed at him.

The room was filled with the pops of a pistol firing several times. Herron was surprised to hear anything at all: a foe as skilled as Sapphire should have drilled him between the eyes, instantly his life cutting to black. But he'd heard the shots, and was still standing.

Sapphire had gone ghostly white, her eyes wide with shock as she collapsed to the ground.

And, once she had dropped out of sight, Shade's pistol was now aimed right at him instead.

7

"Well, isn't this an anticlimax?" Shade said, keeping his pistol aimed right at Herron, his wounded hand bandaged with a kitchen towel. "You know the drill."

Herron tossed the knife, in no position to argue if he wanted to stay breathing for another few seconds at least; it clattered onto the floor somewhere near Sapphire's corpse. The last three people who had worked for the Enclave had been reduced to two... one soon, if Herron was forced to bet on it. There were no more tricks in his kit and no more weapons.

He was at Shade's mercy.

"Spare me the long speech and get it over with," Herron sneered. "I've heard enough bullshit from you to last me well into the afterlife."

"I can end it quickly, if that's what you prefer," Shade replied. "Or we can talk for a little. You might like what I've got to say."

Herron scowled. He'd experienced enough of

Shade's trickery not to expect some hidden agenda, but he had nothing to lose by listening. "Okay."

Shade smiled, raising the pistol. "Treat that as a sign of goodwill. But if you move an inch, I'm going to shoot you between the eyes, got it?"

"Got it."

"Good. Now, the way I see it, you've got a choice. You can listen to my request and accept what I have to offer. Or you can refuse or try to attack me, which means you end up dead."

"Okay. I can't wait to hear what this involves…"

"Your good friends in the CCP hate you, you hate them, and both of you want to destroy each other. That's old news." Shade lazily waved his gun in the direction of Sapphire's body. "But your dead friend there just let the cat out of the bag that my *happy customers* in the CCP also hate me and want to put me six feet under."

Herron snorted, although he was liking where this was going. It might offer not just a chance to keep breathing for a while longer, but also to complete his mission.

"So obviously I'm now feeling a little frosty about my relationship with the regime…"

"And the enemy of my enemy is my friend," Herron finished.

"Exactly. Now they've got my tech and I've got their money, so I could just disappear," Shade went on, as if running through the options in his head for the first time. "But we had a deal, and they've painted a target on me, so I'm going to burn their house to the ground. Send a message about what happens when you cross me."

Herron watched in silence, partly because he knew

Shade liked the sound of his own voice, partly because chipping in might change the assassin's mind while he was still considering his options. He had to let this play out.

"But you're probably wondering," Shade went on, "why spare you? I mean, I'm more than capable of doing this myself, right?" Silence from Herron. "Well, since you ask, this pile of shit is too big for one man – I could shovel it alone, but why should I, when I can get you digging too?"

"All right. So what's your plan?"

Shade smiled, glanced out the window for a second. "See that building on the river lit up like a Christmas tree? It's the new Ministry of State Security headquarters building."

Herron turned his head to look, surprised at how conspicuous – how obvious a target – the building was. A giant, square slab, it was a bright beacon of the regime's authority, a reminder to everyone who lived in the city or who visited the Chinese capital just who was in charge. He wondered if the protestors had tried to get to it, given the MSS would be leading the efforts to crack down on the dissent.

"Not exactly hidden away, is it?" Herron said. "So what, you want to infiltrate the building and take down the MSS leadership?"

"No, I want to kill the leaders, scatter its agents, get my facial recognition technology back, and then burn the building to the ground."

"Ambitious."

"But achievable."

Herron thought about it for only a moment. "I'm in."

Shade nodded, then walked over to Herron and held

a hand out. "We agree to lay off each other until the MSS building is a smoking ruin and we've got the facial recognition technology secure."

"Agreed. But once that's done, I'm going to kill you and take that technology."

"I look forward to you trying. Now, we need to arm up before we leave. The second I show my face downstairs, the MSS is going to realize their little plot has failed."

"I've got guns in the car we could use."

"Not guns as good as mine," Shade said. "And that car is now being watched, so those guns are gone."

Shade headed down the hallway to the bedroom Herron had checked on the way in. He opened the closet, revealing an arsenal that would make any operative green with envy. Herron couldn't hope to carry even a fraction of it.

He watched as Shade armed himself, passing over weapons that could be easily concealed and choosing heavy-hitting items instead. A carbine and a combat shotgun, two pistols, grenades, body armor with ceramic plates... it was an arsenal more suited to a far-off war zone than suburban Beijing.

"You do realize they're going to start shooting at you the minute they see all that?" Herron said.

"Now's not the time for subtlety," Shade said, stepping away from the closet and gesturing for Herron to take his pick of what was left. "We're going *loud*."

Herron held Shade's gaze for another second, then began choosing a similar loadout to Shade. Without knowing what they were getting themselves into, he figured mimicking the Alpha's approach wasn't a bad plan. Switching out one of the pistols for a combat knife, he otherwise selected broadly the same gear.

The only extra things he had were his small, pocket-portable MI6 tech toys – the lock spoofer, the portable jammer, and the mini breaching charges.

They packed the weapons into a pair of large duffel bags, then finished the job by stuffing spare magazines and shells in with them. When they got to the target, they'd transfer the ammo into every available pocket.

Herron stepped back, satisfied they had all they needed for an action-packed evening in China. "Ready?"

"Not quite," Shade said, flashing him a shit-eating grin.

He stepped inside the closet and reached up to the top shelf, taking down a simple cardboard box. It was unmarked, with nothing to give away what was inside or why Shade wanted to haul it with them on the mission.

"A little something to get the party started," he said. "Now we just need to get to my car…"

* * *

IT WAS STRANGE, leaving Sapphire's body at the apartment and taking the elevator down with Shade, after riding it up with her to kill the Enclave Alpha. Not that Herron could dwell on the feeling for long, knowing that on the ground floor they'd find a crew of angry Chinese MSS hitters who were pissed that the pair of them were still alive.

He fed the last few shells into his combat shotgun as the elevator descended the final few floors to the lobby, while Shade slammed a magazine into his carbine.

Together, they would have far more firepower than the MSS goons, but they'd be heavily outnumbered, here and everywhere else they went en route to their target.

And they also had one more challenge Herron insisted on.

"No civilians get shot. The first time I see you gun down one, our deal is off and I'm putting a load of buckshot in your ass."

"You couldn't hit me, even with a shotgun," Shade smirked. Herron fixed him with a hard glare. "Fine, no civilians."

The doors pinged and opened, and Herron emerged into the lobby. As before, plenty of people were coming and going, life in a busy city never fully stopping no matter the time of night. There were just enough people leaning against pillars or seated on sofas to make him wonder which of them were the MSS goons.

"One way to find out," he muttered to himself.

He pointed his shotgun at the roof and fired.

The boom filled the entire lobby, causing every set of eyes to immediately lock onto Herron and Shade. Then, like water bursting from a dam, everyone was moving. Some ran for the exit, some dived to the ground, some hid behind furniture or pillars. Some – the ones Herron was most interested in – reached for weapons.

Shade took care of the first of them, an MSS agent in an overcoat, surrounded by civilians. The Alpha raised his weapon and fired, two quick shots that drilled their foe between the eyes.

Herron was relieved to see that his nemesis was staying good to his word that no civilians would be harmed if it could be avoided, but immediately focused on locating other sources of armed resistance.

Four agents that he could spot. All armed with pistols, all spread out.

Piece of cake.

Shade broke left and Herron broke right, both former Shadow Enclave operatives racing to take cover. They made it behind different pillars as the first of the MSS shots rang out, the *pop pop pop* of their pistols sending yet more civilians running.

Herron remained behind his cover for a second, letting the MSS goons waste their ammo by firing ineffectually. Surprisingly, Shade didn't wait. While Herron considered himself a cobra, waiting for just the right moment before striking swiftly, Shade was more of a sledgehammer. Fearless, even with a bullet wound in his hand, he emerged even as the agents were firing on him, banking on his ability to shoot faster and straighter.

Firing his weapon in quick, efficient bursts, Shade dropped one agent, then another, even as bullets pounded the pillars around him and the wall behind. Only one found its mark, slamming into his vest and earning a grunt of pain, but Shade barely paused. By the time his magazine was empty and he retreated behind cover to reload, three of the operatives were down.

Herron hadn't even taken his first shot.

"Your turn!" Shade laughed as he slammed home another magazine. "But if you need me to bail you out..."

Herron gritted his teeth and moved into the open, shotgun at the ready. To his surprise, the MSS shooter didn't blaze away. While Herron's attention had been on Shade, the man had grabbed a civilian female in a headlock with a pistol jammed against her temple: a human shield. The agent barked in Mandarin, and even if Herron hadn't spent long enough in a Chinese prison to pick up some of the language, the threat was clear enough.

Armed with a shotgun, there was no way Herron could take him out without the scatter shot hitting the woman too.

"Drop it! Drop it! Drop it!" Herron shouted, advancing on the shooter, trying to shock him into surrendering – a suboptimal choice, but the best one he had available. "Drop it *now*!"

His foe did nothing of the sort, clearly aware he was safe so long as Herron wasn't willing to gun down the civilian. To raise the stakes further, the agent shifted his aim from the hostage to Herron, grinning broadly in the knowledge that he'd won...

... until his head exploded, spraying his unfortunate captive and the lobby with blood, gore, and brain matter.

Herron advanced again as the man dropped, grabbing the woman away and shoving her behind cover. Then, raising his weapon, he scanned his surroundings to confirm the coast was clear. Only then could he process that Shade's hyper-accurate shot had saved his life for the second time in an hour.

"I get not killing civilians was part of the deal," Shade said, emerging from cover. "But I didn't think you'd sacrifice yourself to save one..."

"That's the difference between you and me. You think I'm a sucker, I know you're a monster."

"Not a sucker, Mitch, just a little bit of a puss—"

Herron raised the shotgun and unloaded multiple rounds past him. Four armed MSS agents – three men and one woman – had just emerged from the elevators, probably reinforcements from the parking garage.

The repeated boom was deafening, the impact of the shots pronounced. Lacking any body armor, the MSS agents were helpless as dozens of lead pellets tore into them, ripping flesh. Two were dead before they hit the floor, their heads reduced to bloody ruins; the other two went down with devastating wounds to the body. None remained a threat.

Without moving any nearer to the injured agents, Shade raised his carbine and put them out of their misery with single shots to their heads.

"Nice save," Shade said, patting Herron on the back. "Now let's get the hell out of here."

They headed out the front door and into the night. With police sirens sounding off in the distance, they broke into a jog, hauling their duffel bags filled with gear.

"My car's close," Shade said as they ran.

"It had better be," Herron replied. The MSS would be coming down hard for the shit they'd just pulled.

They reached the vehicle a moment later, Herron covering Shade while he stashed their gear in the back seat. A few seconds later, Shade was at the wheel and Herron was riding shotgun.

"You going to tell me the plan now we're clear?" Herron asked. "I don't like surprises."

"Tough. All you need to know is that, for a brief, fleeting moment our interests align. That means you've got nothing to worry about and they've got everything to fear."

Herron opened his mouth to respond, but decided against it. Shade was a zealot, cold and ferocious, and for that exact reason, he couldn't doubt the man's commitment to working together. Until the MSS was destroyed, Shade would focus on nothing but accomplishing their demise, and now Herron was part of that plan.

When the job was done, of course, all bets would be off.

They drove in silence for a half hour. Herron was surprised to find there were fewer checkpoints across this part of the city and seemingly more tolerance for the protesters on the streets. The authorities were keeping back, which in turn meant the protests weren't quite so violent. It was a level of restraint Herron hadn't expected from the regime and its followers.

"Why's it so quiet?"

"This part of town, there's too much prestige on the line. Too much media documenting everything."

"And China doesn't want to appear like it's losing control of its own capital, like it needs to crack skulls to maintain order," Herron said, as the truth became clear to him. "And they don't need to."

"Not thanks to the technology I gave them. They can identify and hunt down the ringleaders of the protests, corral the rest of the leaderless protestors into areas they deem safe, and protect the core."

"The regime's main buildings and personnel."

"Bingo – and that's just where we're going."

A minute later they reached the point of first resistance: a heavy-duty checkpoint with four cop cars, a machine-gun post, and about half a dozen soldiers and cops behind sandbags. There were protesters milling about, but none were approaching the checkpoint, either in vehicles or on foot.

Herron didn't blame them. That machine gun would cut them down instantly.

Shade, however, drove right at the checkpoint, picking up speed as he did so. "Hand me that shotgun. And get ready to bail, fast. You won't have much time."

Finally figuring out what Shade was cooking up, Herron passed him his shotgun, then reached into the back seat for his bag of gear. The assassin jammed it into the footwell, one end braced against the bottom of the seat and the other on the gas. Then, with the car still barreling towards the checkpoint, both men opened their doors and threw themselves out.

Herron landed hard, grunting loudly as his training took over and he rolled to reduce the force of the impact. He felt nothing break, focusing instead on doing everything in his power to keep hold of his bag. When his momentum was spent, he got up to one knee and swiftly unzipped the bag. He plunged his hands in and pulled out a carbine, seeing Shade a few feet away digging around in his kit.

Sighting down his gun, Herron watched as the car got closer to the checkpoint, unstoppable. Even when the troops opened fire with their machine guns, filling the night with the crack of gunfire, it kept on – right until it plowed into the sandbags at the front of the checkpoint.

And exploded.

8

The fireball from the explosion reached high into the air, blowing out windows and causing car alarms to go wild. Closer to the blast, the checkpoint was annihilated – the soldiers killed, the cop cars damaged, and the neatly erected sandbag barriers blown apart. It had gone from being an orderly barrier protecting the inner sanctum of China's leaders to the gate of Hell.

"That's going to leave a mark," Shade smirked, the detonator he'd taken from his bag still clutched in his hand.

"So that's what was in the box..." Herron muttered. "What now?"

"Wait and watch."

In moments, the protesters were surging down to the end of the street, women and men who'd been keeping a cautious distance emboldened by the breach of the city's barriers. Dozens. Then hundreds. As the human tide passed him, Herron saw every second person was on a cell phone, no doubt telling others about the regime's new weak spot, the CCP powerless to hold back the wave unless it started machine-gunning its own people.

As Herron had no doubt it would.

For a regime that had happily smashed dissent for 80 years, another few hundred bodies would be the cost of doing business. Cell phones and media cameras might reduce the chance a little, or increase the blowback, but he was sure the CCP leadership would order its men to fire if it felt threatened enough.

And that would be the real test of the rebellion: would the soldiers fire?

"Brave bastards. Fifty-fifty they'll all be dead in the morning."

"I'd say eighty-twenty," Shade said. "Maybe a hundred percent. But we got them in there."

"Now what?"

Shade frowned. "What do you mean 'now what'? You think we're going to stand around with our thumbs up our asses and miss out on all the fun?"

Herron gestured for him to lead the way, only briefly considering a shot to the back of his head. Now he had an open path to the MSS headquarters, where he'd find the technology he needed, he could easily end Shade and go it alone. Only the fact that he could cause more damage to the PRC with Shade alongside him stopped him from pulling the trigger.

Decision made, he followed Shade through the breach, swept along amongst the horde of protesters streaming into the inner sanctum. So far, these buildings and people had been protected from the consequences of China's aggressive actions both domestic and overseas; now they were facing their reckoning.

The tide flowed for several city blocks, no troops or soldiers to be seen. The central government hadn't expected resistance to get this far, but Herron knew there'd be a response soon enough. For now, the further they walked, the greater the pack of protestors got, more and more citizens spewing through the chink in the regime's armor. Whether the gap in protection would prove fatal to the government would be decided soon enough.

As the crowd converged on Zhongnanhai, the key seat of power for the regime, which was ringed by Chinese police and soldiers, Herron caught up with Shade. "What's the play?"

"Who the hell knows? We've got a thousand decoys. If they come under fire, we shoot back. If not, we'll get inside another way."

Herron didn't love the answer, but he didn't have a better plan. All he could do was keep his eyes peeled for a clue about how the horde of protestors would be received.

Chinese soldiers, standing out front of the Zhongnanhai, started shouting at the protestors. The protestors started shouting back... and kept advancing.

The soldiers held their position.

The protesters put their hands up.

The soldiers shouted warnings.

But didn't fire.

As someone who'd experienced more violence and calamity than most, Herron had never seen anything quite so moving as the unarmed protesters approaching the heavily armed troops. With a single trigger pull, carnage would be unleashed on thousands of people who only wanted a better future for their families and for their country.

But either an order given by a progressive officer or a collective decision by the soldiers themselves meant the dam of authoritarian control over China had cracked. Now, the protesters were in amongst the soldiers, and soon they'd moved beyond them. The history books were being written with each passing second, and yet the ending wasn't yet known.

"Time to go," Shade said, tugging on Herron's sleeve.

Herron nodded, and together they sneaked out the side of the pack, noticed by no one. With each passing second, hundreds more protesters were joining the cause, and as he walked deeper into the regime's so-called safe zone, Herron was surprised to see troops and light armored vehicles with various insignia siding with the civilians.

"It's over," Herron said to Shade, a note of awe in his voice. "They're going to storm the castle."

"Not until we help them," Shade grinned, then pulled the detonator he'd used earlier from his pocket.

"No—"

But Herron was too late. Behind them, back amongst the protesters outside the Zhongnanhai, another explosion rang out, nowhere near as large as the one that had taken out the checkpoint but plenty big enough. A second later, he heard the screams of the wounded and the crack of the soldiers' rifles – the moment of collective unity was over.

Herron grabbed Shade's arm in a powerful grip, furious at himself for not observing that Shade had thrown a small bomb among the crowd. "They were inside, you asshole! You've got them all killed!"

"Some of them, sure," Shade said, shaking himself free. "But I've also focused the attention there while we go to take down the *real* enemy of the people."

He turned away and kept walking, supremely confident Herron would follow.

Herron recalled his promise to the assassin – the moment a civilian got hurt, he'd end Shade's life – but despite the rage burning inside him, and the fierce urge to walk up behind his nemesis and shoot him in the head, he swallowed down the impulse. Shade would get what he deserved, but eradicating the MSS, getting the facial recognition technology, and ending the stranglehold the Chinese regime had over the Chinese people had to be his priorities.

The MSS headquarters was an imposing structure, making no effort to hide its purpose: an evergreen symbol to remind the populace – and the world – who was in charge. From afar, Herron could see there were only two armed guards manning the checkpoint that controlled the road to the building; a token force at best.

"Almost insulting, isn't it?" Shade said.

"You better come good getting us inside," Herron said through gritted teeth. "Otherwise, I'm going to work on the other part of my mission brief first, and figure out how to get your technology back later."

"I've already got the entire Chinese security apparatus focused on the public storming the halls of power, and still, you want more." Shade tutted. "Good thing I've got one last trick up my sleeve."

* * *

PROBABLY THE LAST thing Herron expected to see inside the headquarters for the secret police of one of the most oppressive regimes on Earth was a ballroom.

He supposed even assholes needed to let their hair down sometimes.

Stalking through the cavernous room, weapon drawn, it was hard not to be impressed by its opulence. There were enough tables to seat hundreds of guests, a stage that was currently curtained off, and a large dance floor. It wasn't hard to imagine the regime's privileged few partying here after a hard day squeezing the blood out of their countrymen. Ironically, it had been the dutiful service of those same countrymen who'd provided the weakness that had allowed Herron and Shade – two of the most dangerous predators on Earth – inside.

Shade's ticket to the ball was a key card that granted entrance to the basement of the giant MSS compound, a door left unguarded amidst the greatest turmoil the Chinese capital city had experienced in decades. It was easy enough to understand how the guards who normally manned secondary and tertiary entrances could be sucked away by the maelstrom, but that was still a mistake, given the biggest storm had yet to arrive.

"It's too quiet," Herron whispered, surprised by the lack of armed goons waiting to meet them. "Didn't think they'd be that strapped for talent they'd let us wander in without—"

Gunfire erupted, shattering the elegance of the grand ballroom. Herron's senses snapped into focus, his training propelling him into action. As the crack of bullets echoed through the opulent space, flashes of muzzle fire reflecting off mirrored and polished surfaces, he upturned a table and ducked behind it, Shade doing the same.

"You just *had* to say it, didn't you?" Shade shouted. "In every action movie in the history of humanity, any time the hero says it's a little too quiet, shit gets decisively *loud*."

He raised his weapon and fired back at the dozen shooters who'd revealed themselves at the far end of the room – an ambush that the infiltrators had walked right into. The gunmen were fanning out to continue their flanking move, seeking to surround Herron and Shade in the middle of the cavernous ballroom. They all wielded pistols, which seemed to be the standard tool of the MSS: inferior firepower compared to the carbines Herron and Shade were packing, but quantity had its own quality.

As Shade got to work returning fire, Herron aimed up at one of the grand chandeliers hanging over three of the gunmen. He fired and the light fitting shattered, showering the Chinese shooters with glass. One screamed, wounded, while the others were forced to retreat a little to avoid the falling shards.

Shifting his aim, Herron fired at several of the other shooters, each round carving a path of destruction. His movements were precise, each pull of the trigger fueled by animosity and determination. Opponents fell, their bodies crumpling onto the polished marble floor, their return rounds pounding into the upturned table, failing to find flesh.

Herron mostly ignored the bullets whizzing by, his mind cutting through the chaos, focusing on every shift in the air, every glimpse of movement. He neutralized threats with calculated accuracy, Shade doing the same, a dozen men being cut down for little gain. It was hard to imagine this was the best the MSS could throw at them.

As the final foe collapsed, silence descended. The once majestic ballroom, now devastated, seemed a fitting comparison to the chaos engulfing the Chinese leadership in general. Herron rose cautiously, his gaze searching the room for any remaining danger, but all he could see was a whole bunch of dead and wounded, and Shade.

Their eyes met for a fleeting moment, the tension between them simmering barely beneath the surface.

"Soon, my friend," Shade said, clearly reading Herron's intentions. "We'll get the technology and punish the MSS for putting a hit on us, then we can have it all out."

As they passed the bodies littering the floor, Shade put two rounds into the heads of each of the wounded. Herron kept his eyes peeled, looking behind the vast pillars that lined the path to the exit... and while he didn't seriously expect to find any soldiers cowering there, he was momentarily surprised to spot an MSS officer doing exactly that.

The man was dressed sharply and had row after row of medal ribbons, which told Herron he could get shit done or he got a lot of honorary recognition for doing very little.

Herron leveled his gun at him. "So, nice to meet you. We're going to need your help..." He pressed the pistol against the officer's head. "You in charge of these corpses?"

"I was," he spat. "My best assets are elsewhere. You shouldn't be so proud to shoot office workers to pieces."

"They shoot at me, they're fair game. What's your name?"

"General Kang Qiao."

The name hit Herron like a brick to the head. He'd heard it before, when he'd been imprisoned in a labor camp and sentenced to die. There, it had been spoken in hushed tones by prisoners and guards alike. This was a man so feared that many felt to simply speak of his existence would invite his wrath.

"Well, General Kang, pleasure to finally meet you. Now get your ass up."

Herron took a step back, keeping the gun trained on Kang; the General complied, seemingly docile and obedient despite his fearsome reputation. Waving the gun in the direction of the door at the end of the large hall, Herron indicated where he wanted to go: apparently the only way to proceed deeper into the MSS nerve center.

"Who's this douchebag?" Shade asked, making up the ground between them.

"General Kang."

"*The* General Kang? He's the asshole who authorized the purchase of my facial recognition tech," Shade snarled, "then sicced his attack dogs on me. Probably got your friend killed too."

"Well then, that's handy," Herron said, jamming his gun into the General's back. "Because he's going to take us to his technical team."

"Why?" Kang said, sounding confused, rather than scared. "They can't help you keep the protestors alive outside."

Herron clipped the General in the back of the head with his pistol. "I disagree."

"Fine," General Kang whimpered. "Once we're through the ballroom door, we'll be in the main office area of the Ministry. There's going to be a *lot* of men trying to kill you."

"I have a plan for that," Herron said, shoving Kang forward. "And if you lead us down the wrong path, you're going to eat a bullet."

The General led the way out, seemingly resolved to doing what his captors had asked for in return for his life. As they proceeded into the MSS office space, several MSS agents and staff members appeared in the corridors ahead of them: to each one, Kang barked simple orders in Mandarin.

Back off.

For once, Herron was glad China was ruled by a dictatorial regime with a clear top-to-bottom hierarchy. Everyone knew their place in the pecking order and everyone knew who sat above them. General Kang was top dog, regardless of his status as a prisoner, and even though his underlings might query what was happening, none seemed prepared to draw their weapon and *really* take issue.

Yet.

"Feels too easy," Herron said.

"What did I tell you about saying shit like that?" Shade answered. His voice trailed off, as General Kang stopped at a door. "We're here?"

General Kang nodded. "All of our technical specialists work inside this office. You can let me go now and I will—"

Shade fired a round into his head, spraying Herron with a thin mist of blood. Herron glared at his uneasy ally, who simply shrugged in disdain for the man he'd just blown away. After a moment's consideration, Herron let it go. He might have kept the General around until they were sure they were in the right spot, but equally, he wasn't going to mourn the death of the architect of so much misery.

Quite simply, the world was a much sunnier place without Kang in it.

He stepped over the General's body, pushed the door open, and led inside, pistol raised. They'd reached the technical department of the MSS: the eyes and ears of the most powerful dictatorial regime on Earth, the place people were paid to keep their fellow citizens under control...

... and the final stop on Shade and Herron's magical mystery tour.

9

———

The technical department was large, about half the size of the ballroom they'd just left, with row after row after row of computer terminals manned by techs wearing headsets.

Herron and Shade had entered at the rear of the room, so the backs of everyone inside were to them, giving the new arrivals plenty of time to assess the situation. Large screens dominated every available space on the walls, most of them showing footage of the protests across China, drawn from drones and cameras. One display, however, was zoomed in on the face of a woman.

"Motherfucker," Shade whispered. "That's Li Su, she's one of the main organizers of the protests. She's top of the list of people these assholes wanted to hunt down with my technology."

"I never knew you cared about *anyone* that much."

"I don't. But I also don't like helping people who've tried to have me killed. Let's get this done."

Herron nodded and fired into the air. Every terminal

operator in the room turned as one, and Herron wasn't ashamed to admit to himself he enjoyed the fear painted on their faces. "Don't move a fucking muscle."

Most did as he'd demanded, his instructions obvious even if some of those who didn't speak English. One fool, however, chose not to comply, jumping to his feet and charging at Herron and Shade with a pair of chopsticks in his hand, scattering the remnants of his dinner.

Herron shot him in the knee.

As the man dropped, screaming, Herron called out, "Put one hand up if you speak English."

Everyone in the room raised a hand.

"Well, that's useful." Herron pointed at one of the technicians. "You, help that idiot."

The console operator nodded and ran to the fallen man, who was howling and whimpering in roughly equal measure. He dropped to a crouch, clearly not really knowing how to help a man who'd had his knee blown to hell, but doing an admirable job of putting pressure on the wound to stem some of the bleeding.

He shifted his attention to the rest of the console operators. "Who can lock the door we came in through?"

Silence.

Herron sighed, and opened his mouth to ask again... just as Shade blew out the knee of another console operator. The man went down screaming.

"Don't make my pal here ask again," he bellowed. "You've got thirty seconds, then someone else loses a kneecap."

A dozen or more console operators called out that they knew how to secure the room.

Herron pointed at one of them and nodded. There was a bleep behind him, and when he glanced back, he saw a flashing red light beside the doorframe.

"Can anyone access it from the outside?"

"Only General Kang," replied the panicked technician who'd locked them in.

Herron looked up at the large screens. Although it was hard to digest so much footage and information, he could see the situation in the capital was getting out of hand. The protestors were now inside the Zhongnanhai, the soldiers on duty either refusing orders to shoot or joining in the ranks of the protests.

Elsewhere, on smaller screens, footage from across China was being beamed into the command center. It was clear dozens of cities – including some of the largest in the country and most important in the world – were either under the control of the largest civilian uprising in human history or about to fall to it. There was violence in some places, muzzle flashes captured by drones and fixed cameras, but not everywhere had degenerated into all-out fighting.

"Beautiful, isn't it? Make you want to join the good guys?"

"I'm already the greatest guy," Shade replied. "Now get on with it or I'll shoot you and get my shit back myself."

While Shade covered the room, Herron focused on an operator he assumed was some sort of supervisor. Older and with a more professional look than the squadron of shaggy IT professionals around him, he sat at a console on a raised dais, overlooking the others. They controlled the immune system of the Chinese regime, and Herron hoped this man controlled them.

"You," Herron said, aiming his weapon at the man. "All this needs to stop. Destroy it. Every bit of it. Burn it down to the foundations."

"*Except* the facial recognition system!" Shade chimed in. "Because that'll earn you a bullet as well."

"Like the man said, except the code for the facial recognition you got yesterday. That, you're going to put on a USB flash drive for us to take out of here."

"Impossible," the senior operator said. "If we stop our work, China will be overrun by the barbarians. It might already be too late."

"You're right," Herron said. "It's too late, game's over. Don't be the poor sucker left running down the clock."

The supervisor hesitated, still unconvinced. Herron pressed the barrel of his pistol against his temple. "Not going to ask again."

The man's courage faltered, then disappeared entirely. He nodded, his hands zooming across the keyboard in what Herron figured must be a world record typing speeds. Up on the giant screens, the results were obvious to everyone in the room.

On one display, a drone that had been tracking a hundred thousand protestors in Shanghai lost altitude and crashed.

On another, a status bar displaying the progress of the effort to restore the Great Firewall of China dropped to zero, before the screen went black.

On another, a live effort to censor news on popular social media ceased, allowing a wash of content disparaging to the regime to be posted for the first time.

One after another, the technological tentacles that had helped the regime to maintain its control were hacked off. Combined with the ultimate reluctance of troops to fire on their own countrymen, it sealed the fate of the regime. The whole corrupt, rotten corpse would be ripped apart by millions of angry Chinese citizens, finally able to punch through the sticky membrane that had kept them in their place.

"It's done," the senior operator said, holding out a flash drive for Herron. "All of our systems are offline, backups have been purged, and offsite backups corrupted. And the code for the facial recognition technology is on that stick."

"How can I verify this?" Herron asked, taking hold of the flash drive and pocketing it. "Not that I don't trust you, but... well, I don't trust you."

The operator stared back at him blankly. Herron sighed and looked around for a way to independently confirm the man had carried out his orders. Dozens of other eyes looked back at him, watching and waiting to see what these two American gunmen would do next.

American gunmen.

Herron turned back to the operator. "You got any sort of hotline between the MSS and American intelligence?"

"Yes. But General Kang is the only person authorized to use it."

"Dial it, then hand me the phone."

He waited while the operator carried out his instructions and then handed him a headset. Herron tried it on for size. "Hello?"

"Who is this?" replied a gruff male voice with a thick southern accent, chiding Herron like a troublesome child. "And why the hell is an American calling me on the hotline from Beijing?"

"That's a long story. The short version is: I'm in the

central MSS building and all their technical specialists are currently my prisoners. I've had them wipe all their servers, but time is of the essence here, so I need to know if what they're telling me is true or not. I'm going to need your help to do it."

"I'll bet. But you're not getting shit until you tell me exactly who you are. If this is some kind of false flag operation..."

Herron knew only one way to get the man's instant and undivided attention. "My name is Mitch Herron. Ring a bell?"

There was no response for a few seconds, then a different voice came on the line. "Mr. Herron, this is Bob McGinty, Deputy Director of National Intelligence."

"Shame you didn't get the promotion when your predecessor died, pal. I don't have a lot of time, so are you going to help me or not?"

McGinty responded quickly. "We've run your voice print through our files and it matches. I believe you are who you say you are. My people are working to figure out if your prisoners have enacted your instructions."

"Okay."

"Now, Mr. Herron, listen very carefully," McKinty said, his voice grave. "It's vital nobody in that room be allowed to share that the MSS has a hotline to American intelligence. If you're right, and the crew in that room has carried out your instructions, there's going to be a lot of questions in the wash-up. If the people in that room answer those questions and point the finger at America, it'll start a nuclear war."

Herron winced. McGinty was right. In his rush to confirm he'd achieved his goal, he hadn't thought about the broader geopolitical ramifications of using the hotline.

McKinty was quite clearly instructing Herron to silence any witnesses.

"Understood," Herron said. He had no intention of mowing down a few dozen computer nerds, but he had to stall McKinty until he had a better plan. "Now tell me what I need to know."

"One second..." There was a slight pause, the shuffle of paper in the background, then McGinty spoke again. "We can confirm the Chinese censor network is down and all sorts of shit they'd want to squash is being posted to social media. A list of MSS agents has just been published to WeChat... I'd say whatever magic you worked has gone off without a hitch. The MSS basically lifted its skirt and showed off what it's packing."

"Thanks," Herron replied. "Good chat."

But before Herron could hang up, McKinty called out, "Wait!"

"I'm a little busy here, McKinty."

"Sure, but you're going to want to hear this."

"I'm a little sick of hearing that..."

Herron listened as McKinty said his piece, his eyes widening as he digested the words... then narrowing when he realized what they meant for him. At last, he killed the call, not bothering to acknowledge what he'd heard.

When he'd picked up the phone, he'd thought he was almost done: the MSS was foiled, the facial recognition technology was secure, and only Shade needed to be dealt with.

Now he realized he was just getting started.

He turned to Shade. "It's done. The MSS is finished,

and I've got your tech on that USB flash drive in my pocket."

"Cool," Shade said, then raised his carbine and started firing at the console operators.

Herron screamed out as bullets tore into flesh and pounded computer terminals indiscriminately, devastating both. Those who weren't cut down in the first salvo ran for cover, but Shade coldly gunned them down as they fled.

Frozen in shock for half a second, Herron shook off his horror and ran at the Alpha, trying to stop him before all the civilians were massacred.

He was too slow. By the time he tackled Shade to the ground, the last of the console operators had fallen in a spray of blood.

Both men sprawled to the ground. Herron's head glanced off the side of a terminal on the way down, stunning him momentarily, but Shade couldn't take advantage, his big gun not meant for nimble close-contact fighting.

They wrestled, trading ineffective blows, each man countering the other's attacks, defending or deflecting the worst of the damage. Eventually, Shade gave Herron a stinging backhanded slap that allowed him to shuffle back and climb to his feet. Herron did the same, both men taking a precious second to catch their breath.

"If this is our final showdown," Shade said, spitting a wad of phlegm and blood onto the floor, "I'm not fighting it like brawling schoolboys. Let's try that again."

Herron said nothing, focusing on his defenses as Shade advanced. His enemy struck first, his body a blur of motion as he launched a lightning-fast punch toward Herron's face. Herron's instincts kicked in, and he swiftly deflected the blow with his forearm, countering with a kick at Shade's midsection. Contorting his body, Shade evaded the attack, Herron's foot finding nothing but air.

Both men backed off for a second. By now the room was filled with the sound of MSS agents banging on the door, desperate to get inside. Shade smiled at Herron, whose face stayed stony and grim... then battle erupted again.

Their barrages of strikes and kicks were executed with precision and skill, their techniques flawless, testament to the countless hours they had dedicated to mastering the application of violence. Neither landed a telling blow — nothing enough to wound or slow down their opponent — but Herron was getting all he could handle.

Shade was a little faster, a little stronger, a little more precise. And a lot more ruthless.

Abandoning all martial art, he gave Herron a shove to the chest, driving him back. With a surge of panic, Herron felt his foot skid in a pool of blood, then go out from under him.

"Fuck!" he shouted as he landed hard.

"Pathetic, Mitch," Shade said, unleashing a brutal kick to Herron's midsection. "Pathetic."

Herron tried to get up – staying on the ground meant certain death – but another kick, then another, then another drove all the wind out of him, each hitting like a hammer to his stomach and his chest. A final kick connected with the side of his head, stars exploding in his vision.

"PATHETIC IS WHAT YOU ARE, MITCH!" Shade kicked him again, hard, and Herron curled into a ball as the only defense remaining. "THAT'S WHAT YOU'VE ALWAYS BEEN, THAT'S WHAT YOU'LL ALWAYS BE."

Herron groaned.

"And you know what's most pathetic?" Shade pressed on. "That you hate me because you could have been me."

The words hung heavy in the air, like an invisible toxin, suffocating Herron. He wanted to deny Shade's accusation, but deep down he knew it to be true. He'd been that callous, merciless killer, unperturbed by who or what his masters in the Enclave ordered him to do. It wasn't so hard to imagine an alternate universe where he kept on that path. Kept killing innocents. Kept working for a corrupt organization. Kept becoming more and more like Shade.

But events had taken him off that road, and put him on another, one that led him to annihilate those same bastards who'd exploited him.

"And you could have been me, Shade," Herron said. "You can *still* be like me..."

"Weak? On the run? Without purpose?" Shade sneered, reaching down into Herron's pocket and fished out the USB flash drive and some of the tech toys Herron had stashed in his pocket, then put them in his own pocket. "You're doing such a great job as the poster boy for the good guys, Mitch. Well, you're done now. You can't beat me, and I'm done playing with you."

The blows continued, all the while Herron's mind telling him Shade was right. He'd had multiple attempts to defeat Shade and failed at them all. This last try would yield nothing but his own death.

Except what McKinty had told him on the red line had changed everything. Resisting Shade – meeting violence with force – would only end in his death. Now, Herron had to live.

He rolled away, got to his feet, and ran.

"Seriously?" Shade laughed. "There's nowhere to run, Mitch. You're trapped in here with me. Just accept that this is over and take the loss..."

"You're right," Herron said, reaching the console of the man who'd locked the door for him – a man now lying dead, blood pooling around him. "But you're just as trapped as I am."

Herron pounded the door release.

Instantly, a legion of armed MSS agents burst into the room, guns raised and shouting at Herron and Shade in Mandarin, then in English.

"Freeze!"

Herron fell to his knees, putting his hands up and behind his head.

Shade didn't. Rage in his eyes, he stooped for a gun near his feet.

The MSS agents opened fire and didn't really stop. The man who'd been their savior only a day earlier, who'd provided the technology to keep back the hordes seeking to overthrow the regime, was now a dangerous enemy.

And they'd clearly been briefed not to give him any chance at all.

Shade's body danced with the impact of the first few rounds, as he continued to fight to bring his own gun to bear, but the sheer number of hits ended him before he could fire: a proud lion overwhelmed by a horde of wildebeest.

With one last glance at Herron as he fell, he hit the deck and didn't move again.

Herron breathed a sigh of relief, in pain but alive. The MSS agents swarmed toward him, and he half expected them to gun him down on the spot. With each passing second, his decision to play Chinese Roulette was vindicated. Like Shade, he was known to these men – and their superiors. Superiors who would want to keep him alive for a long time while they extracted the maximum revenge for all the trouble he'd caused them.

Half a dozen agents kept their weapons trained on him, while two others grabbed his arms. Another patted him down quickly and roughly for weapons, in a hurry to get him out of the ops center and away to somewhere quiet so they could rejoin the battle outside. Then, without a word, he was manhandled through the building, passing cubicle farms and meeting rooms, executive offices and lunch areas, all looking the same as offices the world over.

Behind him, two other agents were hauling Shade's corpse.

When they hit the stairs to the basement, he knew this would where he'd most likely meet his end. But if he'd stayed in the room with Shade, he'd certainly be dead. Now, despite the prospect of days of agony, he was still alive.

And that gave him a chance.

10

———

"You've redecorated," Herron said as he picked himself up from the base of the stairs. The guards had decided throwing him down the last few would be fun. "All the blood stained into the concrete really livens the joint up."

In response, two agents picked him up again while another punched him hard, a sharp blow that would have sent him reeling except that he was being held on his feet.

They continued their journey, none of the Chinese agents saying a word, and Herron less keen to antagonize them after that last blow. He'd already taken enough punishment from Shade.

They didn't have far to travel anyway. The torture dungeon wasn't that big: about thirty cells, each with its own heavy steel door. It was dimly lit, with only a few bulbs overhead working hard to illuminate the space. The effect was to make it seem even more horrible for the poor bastards even now moaning and crying behind some of the doors.

"You're lucky we've got enough trouble outside right now that we can't worry about you," one of Herron's captors said as they opened a cell and shoved him inside. "But we'll be back for you later."

"I wouldn't count on it," Herron muttered, even as the pair who'd been following behind his escorts tossed Shade's corpse onto the floor of his cell and then slammed the door shut, leaving him in pitch darkness. "Fuck it…"

He didn't have much of a plan, more the outline of an idea that had flashed through his mind in the second he'd had back at the tech lab. It had a million possible points of failure: the operatives could have shot him dead there and then; they could have searched him and Shade more thoroughly; they could have started the torture right away.

Somehow, however, he'd found himself right where he wanted to be.

He waited around ten minutes, all the time he could bear to spend in this hellhole, then reached down into Shade's pockets. He fished out the USB flash drive and the pair of the small breaching charges he'd transported to the Chinese mainland and had in his own pocket when Shade had ransacked him, a gift from the fine people at MI6.

The MSS goons had missed it in their search, and Herron hoped the charges would be enough to spring him free.

Herron felt around in the dark to get a sense of the door's construction. It had an electronic lock, which he wasn't sure he could blow from the inside of the cell, so he focused instead on the exposed hinges. They were made of heavy-duty steel, but they were his best shot to get the door open.

He prepared the charges – one to each hinge – then activated them. As the thirty-second timer on each started to count down, he upturned the cell's mattress and sheltered behind it. The resulting explosions filled the cell with noise and fire, deafening and hot.

And when it receded, Herron stood.

Crossing the room in the darkness, he shoulder-charged the door, ramming it with all his weight. It gave a little, so he slammed it again and it ripped free of its destroyed hinges, hitting the concrete floor with a thud. Leaving Shade behind for the last time, he exited the cell.

"Come on," Herron said as he glanced at the chalkboards outside each of the rest of the cells, which had the names of those held captive inside written in chalk. One stood out. "Bingo!"

Herron unlocked the door and pulled it open, revealing a room much larger and better-lit than his old cell. Against the wall was a table with various torture implements arranged neatly on it, and in the center of the floor, a metal chair had been bolted, above a drain down which bodily fluids could be easily washed away.

Sat in the chair was Zoe.

She'd been stripped to her underwear and restrained, and looked much the worse for her ordeal. Her gunshot wound had been operated on, but it had been haphazardly stapled closed and left exposed, without even a bandage to keep it clean. A host of cuts and burns on her face and torso told him she'd been tortured extensively.

McKinty had been right: a British agent was in the basement of the MSS building, and Britain was keen to get her back. So keen, in fact, that he'd told Herron that the US Government would get Zoe out of the country if he could get her to the American Embassy in Beijing without the regime finding out, assuming she was even alive at all.

And the deal came with a catch: Herron would have to hand himself in for debriefing, after which he'd walk free.

But he knew that last part was bullshit, because the U.S. had wanted him dead for years...

Still, he'd made his decision.

Approaching her, Herron lifted her chin off her chest. "Zoe? You with me?"

"You left me ..." she mumbled, but her eyes bore into him.

"I had to get Shade."

She coughed. "Did you? Get him?"

"He's dead and I've got the facial recognition technology," he said. "No time to explain anything else, we need to get out of here."

Her cracked and bloody lips curled into a thin smile. "I'm not going anywhere, Mitch. Save yourself and get that tech where it needs to go."

"I'm not debating," he replied, loosening the leather straps binding her wrists and ankles, and helping her to her feet. It was a mistake: unable to hold up her weight, she stumbled to the floor, Herron barely managing to catch her.

"About time I gave you some support," he said, scooping her up.

He lifted her out of the cell, keeping her upright

with one hand while he released the locks on the other cells he passed.

The stink from inside each one hit him in the face like an uppercut. Some of the filthy, impoverished people inside might have been dead, not even looking up at him when he opened the door; others stared, moaned, pleaded, or cried in their own language, as if trying to ward off yet more torture. But he'd done all he could for them now – it was up to them to make their own way to freedom.

At the top of the stairs, he re-entered the hallway of the MSS building, a world apart from the dungeon. He saw nobody, the whole place deserted. Judging from the distant boom of explosions and the flames he could see through windows, the heart of the regime was ablaze, and the legion of workers in the building had either gone to help or run for their lives.

Starting to labor under Zoe's weight, he looked around for some idea of how he – like the office workers – could make his escape. Reasoning from what he'd seen of the building so far, it would have much the same facilities as any other office, he headed for the nearest elevator. The doors slid open as soon as he hit the call button, and he hefted Zoe inside.

A quick check of the floors listed on the panel inside told him all he needed to know. Mashing the right button, he waited for the doors to close and the car to descend.

A moment later, he and Zoe were in the parking garage.

"You've won a new car," Herron muttered to himself, mimicking the voice of a TV game show host. "Now let's hope they're not all locked."

It was a good bet: no car thief in the world would try stealing a ride from the headquarters of Asia's most feared spy agency. Carrying Zoe deeper into the cavernous space, seeking cover amongst the many rows of vehicles, he zeroed in on a black SUV.

Balancing Zoe in his forearms, he tried the rear passenger-side door, grinning when it popped open. He opened it fully, then gently eased her in, laying her across the back seat. She moaned in pain from the manhandling, but soon enough she was resting as comfortably as possible.

Now all he needed to do was hotwire the ca—

Herron grunted as something hit him in the stomach, driving the wind from him and doubling him over.

Instincts kicking in, he shuffled back, bringing his head up to look at whoever had struck out at him. A lone agent – perhaps the only one left in the building – had somehow managed to sneak up on him. Heron cursed himself for being so focused on Zoe's well-being that he'd let his guard down.

His negligence might end up killing them both.

Had the MSS operative just shot him, that's certainly how it would have gone. Instead, the man had wanted to be a hero.

His stomach still clenched in pain from the cheap shot, Herron charged, crashing into the now wide-eyed agent, who'd clearly expected Herron to go down for the count. Realizing his miscalculation, the agent tried to get his pistol out and up.

Too late.

Herron collided with him violently, taking him to the ground like a linebacker hitting a tackle bag.

The agent's skull hit the concrete, and he went limp, knocked out or killed instantly. Herron didn't have the time or the inclination to check: the operative hadn't come alone after all.

A second agent – perhaps the first man's partner – appeared at the end of the aisle, shouting at Herron in Mandarin as he raised his pistol. Faster than his incapacitated friend, he fired from forty yards away, the shots barking loudly in the concrete vault.

The shooter's aim was close but not close enough. As bullets ricocheted around him, Herron snatched up the pistol dropped by the downed MSS agent and disappeared behind cover: the car parked next to the SUV where he'd left Zoe. After checking the pistol's load, he disengaged the safety and took a breath.

The MSS agent would be closing in on his hiding place, but was unaware Herron was armed. Deciding not to meet the other man head-on, Herron rolled under another car, resting on his stomach with his eyes and pistol locked on the road in front of him, braced to shoot.

Five seconds later, as the feet and legs of his foe came into view, he opened fire.

His single shot shattered the shin of his unsuspecting victim, who dropped like a sack of shit to the ground, screaming. As he hit the concrete, his face was turned right towards Herron, pure terror in his eyes.

One pull of the trigger put a bullet between the operative's eyes, ending his threat once and for all.

Wasting no time, Herron rolled out and climbed behind the wheel of the SUV. Breaking open the panel beneath the steering column, he got to work, and hot-wiring the vehicle in under thirty seconds. As the engine roared, he glanced back to confirm Zoe was still alive, then reversed out of the parking space. Then he shifted it into drive, put his foot to the floor, and burned rubber toward the exit.

Outside, there was a short section of clear road before a flimsy-looking boom gate, the only thing between him and freedom.

Herron hit it at sixty miles per hour, smashing it into a million splinters and roaring past the now unmanned security booth.

Back on the main road, he found a few fires burning and the streets clogged with protesters, all chanting in unison as they marched past the soldiers deployed to stop them. It seemed to him that the people had become one huge teeming mass, all pushing for the same change – change that had been a long time coming for the billion-plus people living in China.

"Where are we?" Zoe asked from the back seat, her voice weak.

"In an MSS vehicle," Herron replied. "Headed for the US Embassy."

"They'll kill you," she said, before coughing wetly. "You're the most wanted man in America."

"Doesn't matter. They'll have a doctor ready to help you."

Her protests faded, too weak to stop him. With each passing second, Herron was forced to slow down more as the crowds thickened and choked the roads. The further he got from the political heartland of Beijing, the more vehicles he noticed too, people trying to escape one way while protesters surged the other.

A few times, he saw soldiers armed with shotguns or assault rifles, milling about but doing nothing to stop the flow of people one way or the other. It seemed the People's Liberation Army was living up to its name, helping the people to free China even as the last vestiges of the Party's power – including the MSS – continued to resist.

Finally, the roads grew so badly clogged it was like every car was frozen in time. Horns and raised voices blared, and Herron's heart sank; each passing second mattered, given Zoe's condition, and there was no way the crush of cars and protesters would ease any time soon. He killed the engine.

"Time to go, kid," Herron said, exiting the vehicle then popping the rear door open.

Scooping her in his arms again – and again ignoring her weak, mumbled protests – he walked in the direction of the American Embassy. By now, they were about a mile away, a relatively easy walk under normal circumstances, even carrying Zoe. Fighting against the crush of protesters trying to reach ground zero of the resistance efforts, however, made the journey far tougher.

And all the while, Herron was filled with elation and sadness in equal measure. He was witnessing the collapse of the regime he'd resisted for so long, China's citizens with their eyes wide open for the first time in generations; yet his own eyes wouldn't be open for much longer at all, given the deal he'd cut to keep Zoe alive was likely to cost him his life and his future with Kearns.

Glancing down at Zoe, vulnerable in his arms, was enough to convince him he was on the right path. Years ago, before ending the Enclave and before meeting Kearns, he'd have put Zoe on the cold road and bugged out. It would be child's play – then and now – to evade the Chinese authorities as they struggled against the dissent in their own populace.

But he was at peace with the decisions that had led him here, to the end, because they were his own.

He felt old.

He felt sore.

But, deep down, he also felt proud.

They reached the gates of the United States Embassy a few minutes later. A proud symbol of enduring freedom amongst those currently fighting for liberty, its high walls were topped with razor wire and security cameras, while at the main gate the Marine guard post was so well fortified it looked like it could handle having a nuke dropped on it.

Herron carried Zoe slowly, trying to look harmless to those who'd be tracking his approach on camera even now, and radioing to the guards on the gate. As he got closer, two armed Marines emerged, staying on the United States side of the Embassy entrance; their manner suggested Herron had better stay on the Chinese side of the line.

"Stop right there, sir," one shouted. "I'm going to need you to identify yourself."

"Codeword: Phoenix," Herron shouted back, loud and clear, repeating the phrase McKinty had told him to.

Immediately, the attitude of the Marines changed, from simply cautious to outright hostile. Their grips on their guns tightened, and one reaching up to use his radio while the other kept his eyes locked on Herron, clearly ready to act with lethal force if necessary.

"They want us to bring you in," said the Marine on the radio said. "Her, too."

"She's in bad shape and needs urgent medical care," Herron said. "Provide it, and I'm all yours."

"You're all ours anyway, sir, but we'll help your friend. You'll need to hand her over."

Herron did so, easing Zoe into the arms of Radio Marine, glad the young man in uniform seemed as diligent about her safety and comfort and he'd been. His partner continued to keep a sharp eye on Herron as the exchange took place, having clearly been briefed that the man in front of him was a dangerous individual.

Herron didn't give them anything to worry about; he cared too much about Zoe's safety to give them any trouble. He'd made a deal, now he'd live up to his end of it, giving himself up so that Zoe would have a future. He stood, anchored to the spot, one inch inside China as Zoe was whisked away.

The Marine who remained raised an eyebrow, still holding his gun ready in case. "Well, sir?"

Herron smiled at the Marine, at peace. "Well."

He stepped forward into the future, whatever it might hold, and left his past behind.

On his terms.

EPILOGUE

itch Herron – the FBI's most wanted man and Interpol's third most wanted person – has been killed after a gun battle that started a fire inside the headquarters of the Chinese Ministry of State Security.

While no remains were recovered after the fire, which consumed the entire building amidst the broader downfall of the PRC government, Chinese police commented that Mr Herron is "undoubtedly dead".

When asked for a comment, a spokesperson for the United States Government said: "Mitch Herron was one of the most ruthless killers and terrorists of our time. If he's dead, then good riddance."

Herron was responsible for some of the most high-profile killings and terrorist actions of our time. He leaves no family.

The man sitting outside the Parisian café smirked at the report, folding the paper and tossing it lazily onto the table. With a content sigh, he picked up his espresso and sipped the last of it, before getting to work on the croissant he'd ordered to accompany it.

For a man used to living on the run, in darkness and in shadows, it was an alien sensation to sit in the light, simply watching people go by. It wasn't one he was sure he could get used to, if he were being honest, but it was working for him for now.

That, and something else.

The sunlight beaming on the man's face was nothing compared to the glow emanating from the woman looking down at him from the other side of the table. She'd just arrived after a morning in Paris' boutiques and smiled down at him when he gestured for her to sit.

Just one of countless couples enjoying the eateries in one of the greatest cities on Earth.

She reached over to take his croissant. "Pregnant lady's prerogative. Besides, you don't need it. You're dead."

"Until someone in the U.S. Government changes their mind," he laughed.

Erica Kearns smiled at Mitch Herron. "Well, you're mine until then."

Herron had expected to be killed after handing over Zoe and walking in off the street and into American custody. Because, although the deal he'd been offered was a simple one – medical care and transport out of China for Zoe, in return for debriefing by the CIA about everything he knew – he hadn't expected the U.S. Government to spare him.

But then he'd put the facial recognition technology on the table.

After months of debriefing at Langley – everything he knew about every dark organization on Earth – he'd told the Agency about the technology and that he had his hands on it. Then, after signing the immunity paperwork, he'd told them where he'd stashed the thumb drive inside the U.S. Embassy in Beijing. Once they had it, they'd let him walk.

At last, after years of blackmail and coercion by multiple governments seeking to get him to do their bidding, a government had offered him a deal he could live with. He wasn't sure it'd hold, or if he'd soon have gunmen back on his tail, but it was good enough for him for now.

And for Kearns and their unborn son.

ABOUT THE AUTHOR

Steve P. Vincent is the USA Today Bestselling Author of the Jack Emery and Mitch Herron conspiracy thrillers, and the Frontier Saga science fiction series.

Steve has a degree in political science, a thesis on global terrorism, a decade as a policy advisor and training from the FBI and Australian Army in his conspiracy kit bag.

When he's not writing, Steve enjoys whisky, sports and travel.

You can contact Steve at all the usual places:

stevepvincent.com

steve@stevepvincent.com